THE TOWER AT THE END OF TIME

Amy Sparkes

WALKER
BOOKS

First published 2022 by Walker Books Ltd 87 Vauxhall Walk, London SE11 5HJ

2 4 6 8 10 9 7 5 3 1

Text © 2022 Amy Sparkes

Cover and interior illustration © 2022 Ben Mantle

The right of Amy Sparkes to be identified as author of this work has been asserted in accordance with the Copyright, Designs and Patents Act 1988

This book has been typeset in Berkeley Oldstyle

Printed and bound by CPI Group (UK) Ltd, Croydon CR0 4YY

British Library Cataloguing in Publication Data: a catalogue record for this book is available from the British Library

ISBN 978-1-4063-9532-7

wwww.walker.co.uk

The author will donate 5% of her royalties for this book to ICP Support www.icpsupport.org Reg. charity number: 1146449

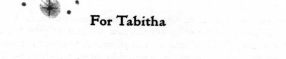 **For Tabitha**

Dear friends,

There's something important I need to tell you.

My days in the House at the Edge of Magic have been the best days of my life. But every journey must come to an end. Even the most extraordinary ones.

I know you'll take care of the most special thing I have in all the world.

And look after my music box, too. It means so much to me.

Please don't try to find me. You know I don't like saying goodbyes.

So, I'll just say thank you. For everything.

CHAPTER 1

If anyone had told Nine a week ago that she would be in a magical house with a hopscotching wizard, a feather-duster-obsessed troll and a stab-first-ask-questions-later wooden spoon, Nine would have laughed in their face. And then picked their pocket.

Yet here she was.

Nine stood in the dark, plum-carpeted hallway of the House at the Edge of Magic, beside Eric the troll – as tall as a man and a half, and like a cross between a tree trunk and a walrus – and a blue and white coat of arms mounted beside the front. It showed two sticks crossed above a large toad, which had a chain-like tongue poking out of its mouth. She had just pulled the tongue out, released it and—

ZA-BAM! Nine had felt a shockwave rock through her body. But it hadn't been enough to shake her smile.

What *was* enough to shake her smile was the sickening lurch which came next.

Nine leaned against the front door. Her brain was surely being sucked out of the top of her skull. Everything hurtled in a direction she didn't understand – but was possibly "up".

"Lady fine?" said Eric in a wobbly voice, as he clung to the end of the banister.

For a moment Nine saw stars in front of her eyes, then they faded away. There was a strange but relieving sensation of lightness, and Nine caught her breath.

"Lady always fine," she said determinedly. Because, for the first time in her life, she should feel absolutely fine.

Gone was her old life as a thief for Pockets, the heartless, whiskery old gang-master. Gone was the dingy, rat-infested warehouse cellar, where she lived with the other thieflings. And this new life, in this strange and magical House, had begun.

Except now the House was flying ... and houses really weren't supposed to fly. In fact, the more she thought about it, the more ridiculous it was. She ignored the rising tightness in her chest and wrapped her arm around the precious satchel slung across her body. This was what she wanted, wasn't it? This was freedom. This was escape. This was a flying house. This was – she really, really hoped – *not* a mistake.

"House free!" said Eric.

"Oho!" crowed Flabberghast the wizard, rubbing his palms together in delight as he skipped up the hallway towards Nine. Behind him skittered a wooden spoon with spindly arms and legs, and a face almost entirely made of two bushy, gingery eyebrows and a large moustache. "Three years!" the wizard continued. "Three years I've waited for this moment! We've visited your world many times, even picked up mortal guests to travel with us, but we've never been stuck there for years before! Freedom from the curse! Freedom from your world! Freedom from your dung-ridden streets!"

"Hey." Nine frowned.

Flabberghast linked elbows with Eric, and the wizard's curly auburn hair bounced about as the two danced around in a circle. Dr Spoon rolled his eyes. Nine looked at the grinning wizard in his indigo pyjamas and fluffy purple slippers and sighed. "Yes, you're welcome."

"Well, naturally, Madam, I am most grateful for your part in the curse-breaking—"

"Which absolutely wouldn't have happened without me."

"—but oh! To travel the realms of magic! To be free once more!" Flabberghast sighed blissfully and his strangely ancient eyes twinkled. Nine couldn't help smiling.

"Now, the Hopscotch Championship is coming up, Madam. That will be our first stop. I've missed three years! And we had best get there early, or we'll never park the House." He wiggled his fingers in excitement. "We should have tea to celebrate." His clapped his hands together again and grinned at Nine.

Eric lolloped contentedly down the long hallway towards the kitchen. Flabberghast followed, pausing to tilt the picture of 'Sir Ignatius the Permanently Late (1589–1641)', one of the many portraits of his ancestors. It hung crooked for a second, then magically righted itself. Flabberghast chuckled and skipped on into the kitchen.

"Fool of a wizard," muttered Spoon, shaking his head. "Now the House is on the move, we can finally find Professor Dish! With the curse broken, perhaps she'll contact me!" He twitched his gingery moustache at Nine, then sprinted up the plum-carpeted staircase to the landing.

Nine had heard so much about Spoon's long-lost partner in alchemy – how Spoon had one half of the formula to change matter into gold, and Dish had the other. She wondered if they'd ever be reunited, and who exactly they were trying to make the gold for. And if they did make lots of gold, surely they wouldn't need it all…?

No, I'm not a thief any more!

"You'll find your room perfectly satisfactory," came Flabberghast's voice, dividing Nine from her thoughts. "The room carefully chooses the guest, not the other way around. Make yourself at home."

"Yes. Home," murmured Nine, the word unfamiliar on her lips. It didn't feel like home...

She climbed up the stairs to the main landing, which had dozens of doors of every size and colour – some small as a mousehole, some larger than a carriage archway. The ridiculously high walls were dotted with hundreds of other doors, all the way up to a distant, ornately painted ceiling.

Some of the doors were reached by rickety wooden steps and landings that doubled back on themselves. Other doors were reached by tall ladders or the huge central spiral staircase that seemed to stretch up for ever. And there were some doors that didn't appear to be reachable at all.

On the right of the main landing, a narrow staircase led to a single small door: Spoon's room. On the door was painted a yellow circle with a smaller circle inside. There was a faint burning smell coming from within and occasional wisps of curling, orange smoke, which tickled the air and then vanished. Nine paused for a moment, then shrugged. When you had a wooden spoon trying to make gold, this almost counted as perfectly normal.

There was a high-pitched creaking sound. Nine looked up sharply as the turquoise door at the top of a tall ladder opened itself just a fraction. *The room chooses the guest, not the other way around.*

As she climbed up the ladder that led to the room, doubts pounded Nine's mind. What if this room wasn't perfect for her? What if she wasn't perfect for the House? What if she was never meant to be here at all? What if this was all a big mistake—?

"Tea cupboard!" warned a distant wizardy voice. Nine paused, mid-climb.

Tea cupboard? Then she understood: the tea cupboard remained cursed and every time someone touched it, there would be a—

ZAP! Nine was a frog with two bushy tails and extra-long arms, clinging to the ladder rung. She had eight eyes, only two of which were open – the rest popping open one at a time, until Nine could see eight ladders in front of her. Slowly, she became unfrogged as the magic faded, and her eight bulbous froggy eyes were replaced by her own, definitely-just-two, eyes.

"I don't think I'll ever get used to magic," Nine muttered, as she climbed up the ladder to face the turquoise door. She reached out to push it open, but before her fingers even reached the wood it began – ever so slowly – to creak open wide. In a tangle of excitement and nerves, Nine stepped inside.

CHAPTER 2

The room was an odd shape, hexagonal but slightly skew-whiff, as if it were stubbornly refusing to be exactly the same as a regular hexagon. The two walls opposite the door each had a tall window, partially covered by a pair of long turquoise curtains. The walls were covered in lilac wallpaper, speckled with golden stars. The floorboards were scattered with thick, woolly rugs, and the softest-looking one lay before a brick fireplace. Nine went towards it, hesitantly, and ran her hands through the long, fleecy material. She thought of the old sack she used to sleep on, the cold seeping through it from the damp stone floor and into her bones.

There was also a wooden chair and writing desk in one of the corners, a wardrobe, a large trunk with a fabric-covered lid and a floor-to-ceiling bookcase full of glorious books. She smiled and trailed her fingers along the gold-lettered spines. They were all strange titles she had never heard of before.

Except…

She stopped at a brown fabric-bound book and her heart gave a little lurch as she read the gold script. *The Mystery of Wolven Moor* by Horatio Piddlewick.

Her favourite book. And the last book she had read in her old life outside the House – taken from the tumbledown library run by dear Mr Downes, the ginger-haired, horn-rim-spectacled librarian. She would miss him more than she cared to admit and yearned to open the book and read a few pages, to feel some sense of normality, familiarity… Her fingers lingered over the title, but she couldn't quite bear to pick it up. To think that, when she last went to read it, the book had been sitting on top of her sackcloth bed. Perhaps Flabberghast was right: the room was perfect for her, after all.

She turned to look at the bed she had now.

A black iron-framed bed, with fluffy pillows, and turquoise-coloured, silky sheets.

A bed. A real, proper bed!

She pushed her homesick feelings aside. There was only one thing to do with a real, proper bed...

Nine took a running jump and threw herself on it. She rolled around, cuddled the puffed-up pillows, then flopped down, star-shaped, on the mattress. The ceiling was painted a beautiful deep blue and was dotted with what looked like sparkling, swirling silver runes.

A house... A home... She had everything she needed. If the room was so perfect for her then why did she still wonder if she had made the right choice?

KNOCK KNOCK.

Nine frowned.

Because the knocking wasn't coming from her bedroom door. It was coming, rather oddly, from her wardrobe.

KNOCK KNOCK.

Nine jumped off the bed and walked over to the wardrobe. As she touched the door handle, she realised where exactly she had seen it before.

And what exactly would be inside. She put a hand on her hip, raised an eyebrow and yanked the door open.

A skull rolled out and stopped at her feet.

"You," said Nine, staring down at the skull. Then she looked at the wardrobe.

Inside, just about propped up, was the un-skulled body of the skeleton. A skeleton in the closet was bad enough, but a headless one was definitely worse.

She had discovered him in the wardrobe during her previous visit to the House. She had learned three things about the skeleton, none of which made her particularly excited to see him again. Firstly, he was gloomy as a grey day in winter. (Though, to be fair, he was dead and stuck in a wardrobe.) Secondly, his finger was really good for picking locks. Thirdly, Flabberghast became oddly flustered when she mentioned him...

"I've been knocking for ages, but I don't suppose you'll replace my head," boomed the skull, without moving his jaw. "No one cares about your head when you're dead. I've been rattled and clattered and thumped about."

"The House took off," said Nine, examining the skull. "By the way, Bonehead, how *do* you speak without moving your mouth?" She tipped the skull upside down.

"Do you mind? Just because I'm dead, people assume they can shuffle me around, *steal* my bones..." he said pointedly.

"That was once. And only one finger," Nine replied, gruffly. "*And* I brought it back. Why are you even in my room?"

"That dreadful wizard moved me here. Said he didn't want me on the landing any more. That I was bringing back painful memories for him. For him! What about me? Nobody cares about *me*. But now you're here, perhaps *you* could bring me out for a change of scene from time to time. Bring a nice cup of tea. Dust my ribcage..."

Nine sighed and plonked the skull back on top of the skeleton. As she did so, it tightened and fused together with a sickening click.

"Sure," said Nine, still trying to work out how she felt about having a skeleton in her bedroom, let alone one who required dusting. "I'll ... um ... definitely dust you later."

She shut the wardrobe door.

"No, you won't," droned the skeleton from the wardrobe. "No one ever dusts me later. Or tells me what's going on outside."

Outside. What exactly was going on outside?

Nine went over to the left-hand window. She rested her hands on the soft turquoise material of the curtains. The House was travelling through magical realms. Did she dare peek? Of course she did. Nine yanked back the curtains.

Blackness. Endless, beautiful blackness. She gasped as swirls of silver strands rose out of nowhere, twisting and dancing together, then exploding in a blinding flash – leaving just a trail of fading stars in the blackness. Then two more swirls of shimmering strands rose, twisted, danced.

"Marvellous, is it not, Madam?" said Flabberghast behind her. Nine spun around to see him smiling contentedly, leaning against her doorframe. He was holding a saucer and sipping from a flowery porcelain teacup. She hoped the skeleton didn't discover Flabberghast was drinking the Finest Tea in All the Realms. The

22

inability to drink tea was surely something else Bonehead had an opinion about.

"We're in the World Between Worlds. In nothing – yet at the fringe of everything. It's one of the most perilous places in existence … but also one of the most wonderful."

Nine put her hand on the window-catch, her curiosity rising. What was it like out there…?

"I strongly advise you *not* to open the window. One guest opened their window and we've never been able to shut it since." He looked lost in his memories for a moment. "Besides, it's safer not to. We are travelling at tremendous speed, Madam."

"It doesn't feel like it," said Nine, looking again at the silvery strands. "It doesn't look like it."

"Of course it doesn't," said Flabberghast, lifting his nose higher in the air. "This is magic of the highest level, Madam. And besides, the House is exceptionally well trained."

WHOMP! A huge shockwave jolted through the House. Nine lost her balance and fell to her knees on the floorboards. She looked up at Flabberghast, who was holding the doorframe with one hand, and his rattling cup and saucer with the other. Tea dripped from Flabberghast's nose onto his pyjamas. His eyes widened in alarm.

"And is this more magic of the highest level?" asked Nine sharply, rubbing her knees as she stood up.

WHOMP! The House jolted. The teacup rattled. Nine fell backwards against the window. It gave an alarming crack but didn't break. Flabberghast fell forwards into the room.

It was one thing to be flying goodness knows where in an unpredictable, magical house. It was quite another to be flying goodness knows where in an unpredictable, magical house when something was going rather ... wrong.

"Ohhhh dear," said Flabberghast, placing his teacup and saucer on the trunk. "This is most unfortunate."

"What?" said Nine, her patience rapidly disappearing. "What is going on?"

"Madam, I do believe the House has hiccups."

CHAPTER 3

"Hiccups?" Nine said. "Why has it got *hiccups*?"

"How would I know, Madam?" said Flabberghast. "Perhaps it's nervous."

"Nervous? How can a house be nervous?!"

"Madam, if YOU were in the World Between Worlds, in NOTHING, at the fringe of EVERYTHING, travelling at tremendous speed, and YOU hadn't flown at all for THREE YEARS because a cold-hearted witch had placed a terrible curse on you, one might imagine YOU'D be nervous, too!"

Nine thought about reminding him exactly whose fault it was that the cold-hearted witch – *his own sister* – had cursed the House in the first place.

"The World Between Worlds is not an ideal place to have hiccups," said Flabberghast, "but I'm

25

confident it will settle down. Until then, we'll just have to be—"

WHOMP! Nine tumbled down onto the floorboards again. She sat up. She was alone in the room. Where was…?

The wardrobe door burst open and Flabberghast staggered out.

"—careful."

"Don't mind me, will you?" grumbled the skeleton.

"Wretched hiccups," muttered Flabberghast, as he quickly shut the wardrobe door behind him and rested his back against it. His cheeks flushed scarlet.

"I suppose there's no *more* damage you can do," droned the skeleton from behind the door. "Although I wouldn't bet on that."

"Damage?" said Nine, looking at Flabberghast suspiciously. "What?"

"Nothing, nothing," gabbled Flabberghast. "No damage here. You know what skeletons are like." He leaned forwards and lowered his voice. "Grumble about anything. Never short of a bone to pick."

"I heard that," grumbled the skeleton. "Which

reminds me. I want a word in your ear about this wardrobe."

BONG! A strange gong-like sound rang out from nowhere, and everywhere.

"*Now* what's going on?"

"Ah, saved by the urn," muttered Flabberghast and leapt towards the door. "Come on."

"What urn?" said Nine, her eyes roving around the room in search of a noisy vase.

"The message urn," said Flabberghast.

"Wonderful. That's really cleared everything up!" said Nine, as they began climbing down the ladder.

On the narrow staircase on the right, Dr Spoon's door flew open. Spoon stormed out, pink-ribboned kilt flapping and his tiny sword drawn.

"What the devil is going on, lad? Is this House dancing a flamin' jig?" he bellowed, with a surprisingly strong voice for a little creature. "I must keep working on my experiments!"

"The House," said Nine wearily, "has hiccups." She suspected this wouldn't be the last time she'd find herself uttering such ridiculous sentences.

"No need for alarm," said Flabberghast. "Everything's under—"

WHOMP! The rungs of the ladder disappeared. Nine hardly had time to realise that her hands and feet were suddenly resting on nothing but thin air before she tumbled down, landing on a satisfyingly soft pile of wizard.

"Oof," it said.

Spoon hopped up on the banister of the narrow staircase, slid down at tremendous speed, flew off the end, rolled into a ball and landed at Nine's feet.

"The House will sort itself out," said Flabberghast, as he and Nine unpiled themselves. "More importantly, we have a message!" For a moment, his eyes sparkled with silvery light.

"If this has anything to do with your blasted hopscotch, so help me," grumbled Spoon, but he followed them across the landing towards the top of the hallway stairs.

BONG! called the message urn from somewhere, this time sounding slightly more irritated. As Nine hurried, her satchel bumped around. A little tinkling sound came from inside it. Her most treasured possession – her only possession apart from her satchel: the little music box she

28

had been left with when she had been abandoned in a doorway as a small child. Before Pockets had seen her and dragged her away.

She reached inside her satchel and clasped her hand around the little silver box. If magic was shooting around everywhere from the hiccups, she wanted to make sure it was safe. She had almost lost it once before, and it had nearly broken her heart. She held it tight as she ran down the staircase behind Flabberghast, her fingertips skimming the handrail. Spoon slid down the banister ahead of them.

"If I were you, lass," he called from the hallway, as they neared the bottom of the staircase, "I'd get down before the next—"

WHOMP! Something like white lightning crackled along the banister handrail, up Nine's arm, through her body, down her other arm, and into the fingers that clasped the music box. It felt as though she had been thumped, and she was thrown violently back up the stairs.

Landing in a crumpled heap at the top, Nine felt dazed.

She instinctively took out her music box and examined it.

Phew. It was fine.

Wait. No. It wasn't fine. It was … whispering?

Nine put the music box to her ear.

Definitely whispering. Why was there whispering? She couldn't make out the words, but there was undoubtedly a voice…

"Come *on*, Madam!" called Flabberghast from the bottom of the stairs.

"I'm trying," snapped Nine, as the wizard dashed off down the hallway. "In case you didn't realise, your banister just sent a bolt of magic through me. And now my music box is whispering!"

"I'm certain it's fine, Madam. Come on!" Flabberghast said as he disappeared down the hallway.

She struggled to her feet, tucked the music box inside her satchel and ran downstairs and towards the kitchen.

The kitchen was cosy but odd. It was crammed with random cupboards of all sizes, with a back door on the far wall. Beyond it was a garden which doubled as a graveyard, and not a place Nine was in a hurry to revisit. On the left-hand side of the room was a crockery-filled dresser and a brick fireplace with a cauldron suspended above, which Eric was dusting with his feather duster. A tall hat stand was on the right-hand side of the kitchen, next to a bucket on the floor, which caught orange gloop dripping from the ceiling.

Also near the hat stand was an arched wooden door, through which – Nine had unfortunately discovered – was a family crypt containing the Sometimes Dead. She was pleased to see the door remained shut, and that the bursts of magic hadn't encouraged the Sometimes Dead into their Sometimes Not Dead mood. On the other side of the arched door was a flowery chamber pot which, Nine was relieved to see, was empty.

Spoon stood on the kitchen table and Flabberghast plonked the urn beside him. It was taller and slimmer than a teapot and was a deep blue, decorated with yellow swirls.

"Message time!" Eric said. He tucked his duster into his apron strap and lolloped over to the others.

"The message urn wouldn't work when the House was cursed," said Flabberghast, "so

I'm terribly out of touch. Another of my sister's thoughtful tricks. Well, let us see who has left a message."

Flabberghast wiggled his fingers in delight then, ceremoniously, he lifted the lid from the urn.

CHAPTER 4

Nine gasped. As though attached to the underside of the lid, the head, shoulders and upper body of an old, grey-haired witch wafted up into the air. Nine stared. The witch was there … but not there. Nine could almost see through her.

Spoon's little shoulders sank in disappointment as he hopped off the table. "Just what we need. Another blasted witch! Why couldn't it be a message from Dish?"

The witch ignored Spoon. "The Hopscotch Championship will be running at the ninth hour of the third day of the seventh month of the tenth moon."

"Tuesday," whispered Flabberghast to Nine.

"Your application has been approved, and you

are cordially invited to participate," droned the witch, staring blankly ahead. "You are cordially invited to participate as your application has been approved."

"I'm allowed to join in," Flabberghast whispered.

"I know what it means!" said Nine irritably. "Who is that?"

"Shhh," said Flabberghast.

"You shhh!"

"Don't interrupt," scolded the witch, flickering her eyes in Nine's direction, then staring blankly ahead. "Congratulations, you may participate, congratulations."

"Does she live in that urn?"

"Shhh," said Spoon.

"Competitors are reminded that this is a glorious but perilous event, so you enter at your own risk in this glorious but perilous event. And don't interrupt," droned the witch.

"How can she—?"

"SHHH!" said Flabberghast and Spoon together, as Eric put his big hands over his mouth and looked nervously at Nine.

The witch huffed loudly. Her dark eyes glowed gold, and a moment later a zap of golden magic shot out from them towards Nine's mouth. Nine didn't have time to scream before her mouth tightened, stiffened – and began to zip shut. Her heart thumped and she made a muffled, outraged noise as her hands flew to her face.

"Madam!" hissed Flabberghast, batting her hands away. "Be quiet!"

Nine glared at him.

"All rules must be adhered to. You must adhere to all rules."

The message witch continued to face ahead, but gave Nine a quick sideways glare. The golden light shot from her eyes again and the zip vanished.

Nine stepped towards the urn. "How DARE you?"

The witch turned her head slowly towards Nine, her eyes glowing ominously golden again.

Flabberghast dashed forwards, cupping both hands over the urn lid above the witch's head. "Yes, yes, thank you, goodbye," he gabbled, slowly forcing the lid down and squishing the witch back into the urn. He clunked the lid on and whirled around to Nine.

"Madam!" he said, his nostrils flaring indignantly. "The Urn-to-Urn Messaging Service was founded by my very own great-great-great-great-great-aunt, Euphemia the Constantly Meddling, and has been delivering messages across the realms for centuries! It is a highly respected service! And the first rule of the Urn-to-Urn Messaging Service, Madam, is that one must never interrupt a message witch! It's terribly rude!"

"*She* was terribly rude! She zipped my mouth up!"

"Understandable," said Spoon. Nine opened her mouth to argue, but Eric reached inside his apron pocket, pulled out a brown-and-white-striped boiled sweet and stuffed it in Nine's mouth. Mostly out of surprise, Nine said nothing, but she bit down and crunched the sweet as noisily as she could, scowling at everyone.

"Anyway, we've more important matters to discuss," continued Spoon. "Like how a blasted Hopscotch Championship is going to help us find Professor Dish!"

"Ah, now you would be surprised, my dear Spoon," said Flabberghast, in an overly cajoling tone. "A gathering of wizards and witches from all over the realms... Seeing things, hearing things... Who knows what information we'll find there?" His face fell for a moment, as if something had occurred to him. "Or who we'll bump into."

WHOMP! Everyone jolted forwards into the table with the next hiccup. Flabberghast's hat leapt off his head, and he jumped up to catch it. As he grabbed it by the rim, a toad fell out of the hat, dropped on Flabberghast's head, then hopped off quickly. Flabberghast tutted and pulled the hat back on.

"So, where does the hopscotch take place?" said Nine.

"Tuesday," said Flabberghast.

"Not when – where."

"Tuesday is a place," said Flabberghast. "If you travel far enough in one direction, it's always Tuesday. A vast improvement actually – the Championship used to be held in the Forest of Endless Sneezing."

Nine frowned. "Was it the forest that was endlessly sneezing or the people?"

BONG! The sound echoed around the kitchen. "More message?" said Eric, glancing uncertainly at Nine, and rummaging in his apron pocket.

Flabberghast fixed his eyes on the message urn. "Who could that be? I'm not expecting any more messages." He placed his hand hesitantly over the lid, then quickly withdrew it. "Hmm. I suggest we do not answer this one."

BONG!! The sound echoed louder, more impatient. The urn began to vibrate, rocking slightly from side to side, the lid chinking against the body. Nine stared at it, her fingers itching and twitching to touch it. Curiosity was both her gift and her curse, which was precisely how she had ended up in the House in the first place.

Just one quick peep…

BONG!!!

Just one…

The urn rocked violently from side to side.

…quick…

Flabberghast took three steps backwards. "Madam, I strongly advise—"

"Yes, I'm sure you do," said Nine, stepping forwards. "But we both know I never listen to *you*."

And she lifted the lid off the urn…

CHAPTER 5

KABOOM! There was a small explosion from inside the urn, with a puff of mauve powder and a stomach-churning smell of rotting vegetables. The lid was lifted out of Nine's hand as she was thrown backwards beside Flabberghast, landing hard on the flagstone kitchen floor. Her heart thumped as she watched a wide band of mauve light shoot furiously upwards, taking the urn lid along with it. Then there was silence, except for a slight *chink* as the lid touched the ceiling.

"Madam, you seem incapable of not touching things I tell you not to touch!" said Flabberghast, pulling Nine to her feet.

"Then stop telling me not to touch them!" Nine shot back.

They both turned back to the message urn, as the mauve light began to transform into the features of a huge, thin person, their torso unnaturally stretching from the urn on the table up to the kitchen ceiling. The light faded and revealed a boy slightly older than Flabberghast, with a similarly ancient feel about him. His hair was wavy and down to his shoulders, blond with a strong greenish tinge. His thin-lipped face had a strange mauve colour, and his pinky-purple eyes narrowed as he loomed over them.

"Friend of yours?" said Nine, as Flabberghast gulped beside her.

"When you say 'friend'..." squeaked Flabberghast. He straightened up, plastered on a smile, threw his arms wide and bobbed in a strange curtsey.

Spoon drew his sword from its sheath. "Who the devil is this?"

"Ah! Gazillion the Unstoppable. How – how *are* you?" said Flabberghast, standing upright again.

"I," boomed Gazillion in a strong but nasal voice, "am not a turnip."

Nine sighed. In every sense she could think of,

this was not a promising start.

"No! Clearly you are not," said Flabberghast, the flicker of fear in his eyes betraying his fixed grin. "Congratulations on your un ... turnipping. You look decidedly un ... turnipped."

"UNTRUE, Flabberghast the Unworthy!" bellowed Gazillion.

"Unworthy?" said Nine, turning to Flabberghast, who flushed scarlet.

The huge, translucent figure bent forwards, bringing his furious face nearer to them. Nine and Flabberghast shuffled closer together. "Look at my erstwhile beautiful hair! It's green! And my gorgeous face! Purple!"

Nine rolled her eyes.

Wonderful. Another wizard with all the charm of a pile of dung.

"Oh ... I ... I wouldn't say *purple*," flustered Flabberghast, "rather more ... pinkish ... a glowing complexion!"

"FOR A TURNIP, YES!" bellowed Gazillion, bending over so far that his mauve-ish nose almost touched Flabberghast's. "I do not like being turned into a vegetable. I do not know for certain *who* turned me into a vegetable. But I am going to find out. Law of Magic, Rule 37853, Flabberghast."

Nine looked at Flabberghast out of the corner of her eye. She was fairly sure he was holding his breath.

"I heard rumours your House had been released from its curse. The others thought it was a shame, but I " – he smiled threateningly – "could not be more delighted."

WHOMP!

Everyone jolted again with the hiccup and the urn rocked backwards and forwards. The hugely tall Gazillion wobbled around like a surprised, overstretched jack-in-the-box. Gazillion regained his balance. His eyes shot left and right suspiciously. "Has your House got hiccups?"

"I believe so, yes," squeaked Flabberghast.

"Good luck with that. They're nigh on impossible to shift," said Gazillion lightly. Then his face returned to its sneering, menacing look and his voice recovered its sneering, menacing tone. "I'm going to find out exactly who turned me into a turnip, Flabberghast. I'm going to defeat the hopscotch grid, enter the Tower at the End of Time and ask my question. And the Tower, Flabberghast, never lies. See you at the Championship."

He zoomed back down into the urn at an alarming rate.

The lid gave another *chink* as it clattered down onto the urn.

Spoon sheathed his sword again as Nine looked at Flabberghast, who sank to his knees.

"Wizard cross," said Eric, his eyes wide.

Nine turned to Flabberghast. "Just tell me," she said through gritted teeth, "that it wasn't you. Tell me you didn't turn him into a turnip."

Flabberghast leapt to his feet. "Well, you've met him, Madam! He deserved it!"

"You lied!" said Spoon. "You're Flabberghast the Unworthy? You said you were called Flabberghast the Great!"

The wizard whirled around so forcefully, that Nine stepped backwards. "I will be," he said, his fingertips sparkling silver, "when I win the Championship."

"But this Law of Magic, three … seven… What's that?" said Nine. A sense of unease prickled her.

44

"*No witch or wizard may turn another witch or wizard into a fruit or vegetable.* If you are found guilty at your trial..."

"What?"

"You face the same fate," said Flabberghast. "Being transformed into a fruit or vegetable."

Nine sighed. "And he's going to this Tower at the End of Time."

"Apparently so, Madam!"

"Which honestly answers any question you have."

Flabberghast squirmed. He dashed towards the table and grabbed the urn. "Well, only if you reach the Asking Stone in the Tower."

"Asking Stone? What Asking Stone?"

"It was created by Hildegard the Ridiculously Knowledgeable. She became so fed up with being asked for advice, she filled the Stone with her knowledge and wisdom and placed an honesty charm upon it."

"And the Tower?" asked Nine.

"Well, people were so impressed they built a shrine for the Stone. Except the Stone was so knowledgeable it infiltrated every fibre of the Tower's construction. It *became* the Tower, Madam." Flabberghast tucked the urn under his arm, one hand clasping the lid shut. "If you ask me, the power rather went to its head. Even Hildegard went to ask the Tower what she should do – it told her to retire by the sea and take up stamp collecting, because it was clearly better than she was."

"Well, I have a question for this Tower!" said Spoon. "Why are we going to watch flamin' wizards skip around instead of finding Dish?" He wiggled his fingers and skipped mockingly on the spot, his kilt flapping.

Flabberghast said nothing, but marched over to a collection of different-shaped cupboards near the cauldron. Nine watched as he opened a short, narrow door and hurled the urn inside. "Why did you do that?" said Nine, as Flabberghast slammed the cupboard door shut.

"I don't believe we need any more messages today," he said. A look of grim determination came over his face as he headed for the kitchen door. "I should start practising. Hopscotch is a matter of honour and pride."

"Aye," said Spoon. "And *you'd* better grab those when you can, Flabberghast the Unworthy."

Flabberghast glared at Spoon. "I'll prove that I am *not* unworthy. I will *not* miss the Championship this year. Not for anyone or anything."

Spoon clenched his tiny fists and roared in frustration. His wooden face turned red and Nine wondered whether it was actually possible for a wooden spoon to explode. Then, in a rush of fury, Spoon sprinted over to the flowery chamber pot sitting by the arched doorway to the Sometimes Dead. Despite his spindly arms, he lifted it above his head and then dashed it down onto the flagstone floor, with an almighty smash.

"HOW DARE YOU!" bellowed Flabberghast. "I liked that chamber pot!"

"Aye! You have so much in common!" Spoon shot back. "Usually both filled with utter—"

"Oi!" said Nine, as Spoon somersaulted in the air and snatched Flabberghast's hat from his head. He clambered up to the top of the hat stand.

WHOMP. As the House hiccupped again, the hat stand began to whistle cheerily.

"Give my hat back!"

"NO!"

Eric reached into his apron pocket and desperately offered boiled sweets.

Instead, Flabberghast grabbed the feather duster tucked into the troll's apron, ran to the hat stand and jabbed the duster at Spoon like a sword.

Spoon jabbed his sword back.

"Friends cross," wailed Eric. "Lady fix?"

"We can't waste time on a blasted hopscotch contest when we should be looking for Professor Dish. I owe someone the secret formula! I told you I have the devil on my tail," raged Spoon, as Flabberghast shook the hat stand, trying to dislodge the irate utensil. "Oh, you're the most useless wizard I've ever met!"

"I'll show you who's useless!"

Flabberghast tossed Eric's feather duster aside. The whistling hat stand helpfully sprouted a wooden arm and caught it. Flabberghast stretched out his fingers. The tips sparkled silver...

"Do. Your. Worst!" growled Spoon.

"With pleasure!"

This was the home, the family, Nine had longed for. But everything was falling apart. She

48

was starting to wish she'd never heard of the Hopscotch Championship, but there was about as much chance of talking Flabberghast out of it as persuading Spoon to take up knitting. She marched over and grasped the hat stand with both hands.

"Will you sort everyone out!" she shouted.

Two more long arms shot out of the hat stand. One reached up, grabbed Spoon, and dangled him upside down, still waving his sword and the hat. The other grabbed Flabberghast by the back of his pyjamas and held him a few feet above the ground.

Nine smiled smugly until there was a whoosh of movement, another arm, a grip of wood on ankle, and Nine was also upside down, with her nose a few inches away from the floor.

Silence. Except for the cheery whistling of a hat stand.

"Lady fix!" beamed Eric.

Everyone looked at everyone. Then everyone glared at Nine, who wondered if she should have thought about the next part of the plan. Eric leaned over and put his head next to Nine's.

"Lady stuck?" asked Eric uncertainly.

"No," said Nine. "I'm thinking."

WHOMP! Another hiccup.

The hat stand let go of everything it had been holding, its arms disappearing back into the wood. Flabberghast, Nine and Spoon tumbled to the floor. A feather duster landed on Nine's head.

Flabberghast snatched his hat from Spoon and plonked it angrily on his head.

"Hopscotch first," said Flabberghast. "Then I'll ask the Tower where to find her. We will find Professor Dish. You have my word."

Spoon scowled. "Your word means nothing, wizard."

"You do not understand. It's essential that I attend the Championship. There will already be shame heaped upon me for missing three years," Flabberghast sighed. "Gazillion will take great pleasure in informing the judges that the curse is lifted. My presence is expected. If I do not attend, they will think me afraid. They will think me a failure."

He lowered his gaze for a moment, and Nine

shuffled uncomfortably. This was not the ranting, boasting wizard she knew.

"And shall we say, their opinion of me is not particularly high to begin with." Flabberghast's eyes looked a little watery. "I must go."

Flabberghast marched down the hallway, followed by Nine and Spoon. He stormed into his study, slamming the door behind him. The moment it was shut, the door melted away into what seemed to be nothing. Something like raindrops ran down where the door used to be. Nine leaned forwards, fingers outstretched, curious to touch the rain, but then suddenly a fiery, vertical hopscotch grid appeared in its place.

Nine gasped and quickly stepped back, watching as number one appeared as a single square at the bottom, then two and three as double squares, then four as a single, all the way up to number ten as a single square at the top. The outline of every numbered box burned with golden fire, which ran along the lines like an angry current, crackling and spitting.

Nine frowned. She had watched children play

hopscotch when she'd lived in the world outside the House. And it didn't usually involve fire...

"Think twice before you ever enter that room, lass," said Spoon, stabbing his sword into the carpet. "Stepping inside that study is stepping inside the boy's mind. And I tell ye, that's not for the faint-hearted. Now I need a cup of tea before I stab someone whose name starts with Flabber and ends with ghast!"

He plucked the sword out of the carpet and stormed towards the kitchen, leaving Nine staring at the blazing hopscotch grid.

The Tower at the End of Time ... the Asking Stone...

Maybe Nine had a question of her own.

She reached for the now silent music box inside her satchel and held it in her hand. Little fingers of fire flickered out from the hopscotch grid, as if they were reaching for the music box. Nine's heart thumped, as the twisting, fiery fingers came closer ... closer...

ZAP! Nine had a curly purple tail, two heads, and was light as a feather. She zoomed upwards to the hallway ceiling. At the little burst of magic from the still-cursed tea cupboard, the flickering fingers retracted into their fiery squares.

"Oi!" Nine bellowed to Spoon in the kitchen, as she hovered with one hand against the ceiling. "Call 'tea cupboard' before you touch the tea cupboard!"

"Tea cupboard!" snapped Spoon's distant voice.

Nine tutted as the curse wore off and she zoomed back down again, tucking her music box back into her satchel as she did so.

"I'm not ready to be inside Flabberghast's mind," she said, staring at the fiery grid. "But I am definitely ready for a cup of tea."

CHAPTER 6

A strange smell wafted through the kitchen doorway. Earthy, peppery ... and something she just couldn't quite put her finger on.

Eric was frying a strange-smelling concoction in an iron pan. His apron had ominous grey splodges on it, and Nine began to fear this might be breakfast.

"Lady eat," said Eric. The corners of his mouth were downturned, and his forehead was wrinkled with frowns. "Pancake help."

"Oh," said Nine, walking over to the table. This was not good. "Good."

Eric flipped what was probably meant to be a pancake up in the air. He caught it again and gave a little cheer. Nine looked at the ceiling above

Eric, where at least three grey pancakes were splattered. One was partially peeling off.

"I would nae touch them if I were you," said Spoon. "Even with the best cookery book in the realms that troll could nae make decent pancakes." He was sitting at the wooden table in the middle of the kitchen, sipping delicately from a china cup – but still looking like he was thinking wizard-stabbing thoughts. Nine joined him at the table, on which were laid a teapot, more cups, saucers and the sugar bowl. There were two bright pink, palm-sized ball-looking things with thick, dimpled peel and short, soft spikes. Spoon picked one up and munched it angrily. He rolled the other to Nine.

"What is it?" asked Nine, prodding it cautiously in case it was going to bite her.

"Some kind of fruit from the conservatory – and better than what's coming, lass."

Nine watched with concern as Eric loaded plates of rolled pancakes onto a tray. She quickly bit into the fruit – zingy, with definite undertones of old sock. It was strangely filling, and she gobbled it quickly. Nine grabbed a cup and saucer and filled the cup from the teapot. She took a sip and immediately felt a little calmer.

Strawberry tea... The Finest Tea in All the Realms...

"All he cares about is hopscotch," sighed Spoon. "This Tower had better tell us where to find Dish. She's my partner – my friend. Too long we've been apart now."

Nine frowned. "So, Dish has half the secret for how to turn things into gold. And you have the other half?"

"Aye," said Spoon. "It was a brilliant idea to share it between us – until we got separated." Then he yelled towards the study, "AND UNTIL I HITCHHIKED A RIDE WITH A RIDICULOUS WIZARD WHO GOT HIMSELF CURSED BY HIS SISTER AND STUCK IN A HOUSE FOR THREE FLAMIN' YEARS." He looked at Nine darkly. "And I tell you, lass, three years is a long time for a person to wait when you've promised them the answer. Especially if that person does not like waiting."

"Who? Who is waiting for the answer?"

"She is shrouded in mystery. Only Dish knows, and she would nae tell me."

"What will happen when you give this person the secret?"

Spoon took another sip of tea. He looked at Nine and narrowed his eyes. "My debt will be paid. What happens after that is no concern of mine, lass."

WHOMP! Another hiccup. The chair Nine was leaning on suddenly vanished, causing her to lurch into the table. The music box whispered again. Nine pulled it out of her satchel and cradled it thoughtfully. "The hiccups are getting stronger."

"Lady eat. Lady like," said Eric, plonking the plate of grey pancakes in front of her, before trotting happily back to the cauldron. Nine stared at the pancakes doubtfully, then gulped down the rest of her tea.

WHOMP! Nine's chair appeared again as the House hiccupped. She pulled it out, sat down at the table, then picked up a rolled pancake and cautiously nibbled.

"Mmmm," she said, frowning. "What exactly is in this pancake, Eric?"

"Nice pancake." The troll smiled proudly as Nine stuffed some more into her mouth. "Bone pancake."

At that moment, Nine crunched on something hard that made her jaw judder. She froze. Nine waited until Eric's overlong toenails scraped back across the floor to the cauldron, then spat the pancake out onto her plate.

"If there's one thing I've learned in this ridiculous house, lass," grumbled Spoon, "it's that you *never* eat the pancakes."

They both peered at Eric, humming by the cauldron. The just-about-stuck-on-the-ceiling pancake peeled off and splatted onto the troll's head.

WHOMP! The entire table and all its pancakes disappeared. Nine breathed a sigh of relief.

WHOMP! The chairs disappeared and Nine and Spoon fell on their bottoms.

But this time, something felt strange. Well, stranger than usual for a magical house with hiccups. Nine felt like her stomach had been twisted inside out and her brain had jumped from her head. Judging by the dazed and worried expressions on Spoon's and Eric's faces, she guessed they felt the same.

"That was ... different?" she asked.

Flabberghast came hurtling into the kitchen so fast his hat almost fell off. His eyes were wide and he looked worried. The wizard headed straight for the kitchen dresser and got down on his hands and knees. He opened the cupboard door and stared inside.

"Ohhhh dear," he said grimly.

Eric and Spoon scrambled over on their hands and knees and looked inside the cupboard.

"What now?" said Nine. "Why are you staring into a cupboard?"

"We're not," said Spoon, as they continued to stare into the cupboard.

Nine tutted loudly and crawled on her hands and knees beside Flabberghast. He huffed at her as she deliberately budged him over, then peered inside.

"Oh," she said, trying and failing to keep the surprise from her voice.

Because a huge, green, reptilian eye was staring back at her.

CHAPTER 7

The eye was surrounded by blue, scaly skin and appeared to be looking in through a window at the back of the cupboard.

"Something's looking at us," whispered Nine.

"Yes, Madam," said Flabberghast sharply, with increasing panic in his voice. "I am aware of that! And it's not meant to be there. Or, to be more precise, *we* are not exactly meant to be *here*."

"Where?"

Flabberghast gulped. "I'm not entirely sure."

"You're not entirely sure where we are but we're not exactly meant to be here."

"I fear so," said Flabberghast.

Oh, good grief.

Nine shifted her gaze from the reptilian eye

and frowned at the ridiculous wizard. Prickles of irritation crawled up her spine and tickled her brain. "What just happened? Why is there an eye in the cupboard?"

"Not cupboard," said Eric. "Window."

"Well, why is there a WINDOW in the cupboard?!"

"Obviously, because it was the best way to spy on the green-horned minotaurs when they were attacking," said Flabberghast.

"Obviously," said Nine. She frowned back at the unblinking eye. "So, there's a big eye in the World Between Worlds. Where are the sparkly, twisty things?"

"Where, indeed," said Flabberghast. "And therein lies the problem, Madam." He looked at her, his face pale. "I do not believe we're in the World Between Worlds any more."

Nine stared at him blankly. "Then … where are we?"

"Regretfully, I have no idea."

WHOMP! The table and chairs reappeared. Nine felt the same stomach-twisting, brain-jumping, lurching feeling as the four of them tumbled into each other on the kitchen floor. The hat stand whistled again.

"And why does that hat stand keep whistling? It's giving me a headache," grumbled Nine, rubbing her aching, brain-jumped head.

"It's the tune Great Uncle Marvin used to whistle many years ago," said Flabberghast, staring into the cupboard again. "It always pipes up when there's a bit of extra magic being thrown about. Presumably the magical surge, in this case from the hiccups, releases an energetic memory which the object has retained."

"And your hat stand remembers the tune…?"

"Yes, Madam! Apparently so!"

"An energetic memory thing?" A little spark lit up in Nine's heart. "That could be why my music box is whispering!"

"Madam, please be silent! We have more pressing matters at hand!" said Flabberghast, pointing at the cupboard. "Look!"

Nine peered inside and gasped. The eye had gone, and outside the window there was now a snow-covered landscape. White mountains, sleeping trees… But most beautiful of all were the many softly glowing snowflakes. They were huge, bigger than Nine's hand, and floated all around.

"They've got *faces*," said Nine, as one of the snowflakes drifted towards them. She stared at the delicate face, the glowing eyes now meeting her gaze. It floated closer, nearly at the windowpane. "They're beautiful."

Suddenly, the snowflake's face changed. Its eyes narrowed and its mouth opened unnaturally wide, almost filling the window, as it bared rows and rows of razor-sharp icicle teeth. It screeched an ear-splitting, blood-curdling cry.

"AAARGH!" yelled Nine, Flabberghast, Eric and Spoon, scrambling away from the window. Nine slammed the cupboard door shut.

WHOMP! The House rocked again. Stomach-twist. Brain-jump.

Everyone and everything began to float. Nine scrabbled at the air, pointlessly.

"Why were there snowflakes?" demanded Spoon. "What the devil is going on?"

"The hiccups are getting stronger. I fear they are not only causing magical surges inside the House, but are now causing us to bounce in and out of worlds as we pass," said Flabberghast, warily eyeing the bucket of orange slop floating towards him. "This, I fear, is not good news."

"So where are we now?"

"You're nearest the window, Madam." Flabberghast pointed at the wooden dresser floating behind Nine.

She grabbed hold of it and edged herself towards the cupboard door, then opened it and peered inside.

"Just bubbles," she said, staring in amazement at the hundreds of bubbles floating upwards. "We're in a bubble world! They've got pictures in them!" A bubble came up close to the window, and she saw a reflection of herself, staring back. A tiny Eric was reflected inside the next bubble.

"Eric fly!" said the delighted troll behind her.

Nine looked over her shoulder and couldn't resist a smile at Eric, flapping his huge arms in delight yet failing to move anywhere.

"Eric fly!"

"Oh, this is impossible!" groaned Flabberghast, clutching on to a passing kitchen chair. He tutted as his hat floated off towards the fireplace.

"*You* think it's impossible?!" said Spoon sharply, putting his spindly arms on his kilted hips as he floated in a cartwheel above Nine, missing the upside-down hat stand by an inch. "How can I conduct my experiments under these conditions?"

Flabberghast narrowed his eyes suspiciously as the bucket of orange slop passed directly overhead.

WHOMP! Stomach-twist. Brain-jump.

There was a noisy clattering of wooden furniture landing on flagstones, a rattle of crockery landing on dresser, a thump of bottoms landing on chairs, and a satisfying plop of orange slime landing on wizard.

"Enough!" barked Flabberghast, tossing the bucket from his head and wiping the slime from his face. "This is intolerable! These hiccups must be cured!"

"No fly," said Eric sadly, perching on the table. He flapped his arms hopefully and jumped down from the table with a very un-flying thump.

"Madam! I know what to do! Or rather ... where to *find out* what to do. There is a book,

Magical Houses and How to Tame Them by Grimlock the Indomitable," said Flabberghast, leaping up from the chair. "I borrowed it from the library when we had an infestation of flying frogs in the nut trees. I didn't return the book right away – the library was having rather a bad day. The book's still in the conservatory. First floor, green door. And watch out for the starflower – it nibbles a bit."

"*Nibbles?*"

"Just a bit. Now make haste, Madam. And take this confounded bucket with you and out of my sight," Flabberghast shoved the bucket into Nine's hand and tried to push her towards the kitchen door, but Nine wriggled free.

No one would push her, thank you very much.

"Why don't *you* go?"

"Ah, well, it's all very hot and uncomfortable in the conservatory and besides … I have an allergic reaction to the Winter-Blooming Wart Bush." He whispered to Nine behind his hand, "I come out in winter-blooming warts."

"Oh, for goodness' sake." Nine sighed and headed for the hallway, swinging the bucket irritably and sending orange droplets flying.

"*Magical Houses and How to Tame Them*, by Grimlock the Indom … Indom…"

"In-dom-it-a-ble," came Flabberghast's voice.

"I'm going to write a book," Nine called over her shoulder. "*Wizards and How to Get Rid of Them* by Nine the Downright Irr-i-tat-ed."

CHAPTER 8

Nine reached the landing and scanned the jumble of doors. There it was – the very last door on the right-hand side! She dashed towards it, admiring the outlines of delicate golden leaves etched into the green paint. Nine clasped the golden door handle...

Find the book, grab the book, leave. It can't be as bad as the library.

All the same, she twisted the handle cautiously and peeped around the door.

A wave of airless heat hit her as she stepped into the room. Flabberghast was right – it certainly was hot and uncomfortable. The intense heat made her feel prickly and grumpy already. She put down the orange slop bucket and looked around.

An arched glass ceiling and windows extending from floor to ceiling. It was filled with plants and flowers of different shapes and sizes, crammed into colourful pots around the room. Some were tall, thin and spiky, and there were small trees bearing the bright pink spherical fruit she'd eaten. An odd black-leafed plant smelled worse than Eric's pancakes.

There was an ominous rustling sound behind Nine, but whenever she spun round to check, there was silence and stillness, apart from some suspiciously wobbling leaves from a thick ivy climbing the wall.

Nine was used to being on her guard in this House, and didn't trust any of the plants as far as she could throw them. Which, in the case of the huge, star-flowered plant in front of her, wouldn't be very far. Rooted in a large pot, it had a thorny stem as wide as her body and was so tall, that the golden and strangely pollenless star at the top brushed the glass ceiling. She gave it a steely glare.

Now, where was that book? If only Mr Downes were here, with his librarian's instinct for finding lost books...

He would have been horrified at a book being left – out of place – in a conservatory, especially one where there were plants that apparently had a tendency to bite or bring you out in winter-blooming warts. Dear Mr Downes, with his notebook and his permanent exasperation with Nine. But he had saved her. In every possible way she could think of, he and his library had saved her...

Back home... Perhaps she should never have left.

Nine's throat tightened and she pushed away the memory of the librarian and his library. This was her home now. Wasn't it...?

WHOMP! Stomach-twist. Brain-jump. Where were they now?

Nine moved through the thick forest of plants, past a large, puffy cactus, towards the windows of the conservatory. She pressed her hands against the glass and looked outside. The House was flying through a peach-coloured sky above a rocky, lifeless landscape.

As Nine turned back around, she noticed a thin-legged table on the other side of the conservatory, poking out from a bush with hundreds of tiny flowers. As she walked towards it, she saw a dark green book on the table, with worn golden letters on the cover. *Magical Houses and How to Tame Them* by Grimlock the Indomitable. She reached out her hand. That was all she needed. Now she could—

Out of the corner of her eye, Nine saw something small whizzing towards her. Quickly, she moved away from the book just as a needle-sharp spike the length of her hand harpooned the table.

She looked in the direction it had come from. The cactus by the window was changing colour from mellow green to a rather alarming purply-red. It looked like it was tensing, drawing itself in. Then, as if it were puffing out in relief, it deflated back to its normal size as about twenty razor-sharp spikes came shooting towards the table.

Nine gasped as she quickly leapt forwards and grabbed the book. She held it up like a shield as a handful of spikes pierced the cover of the book, landing upright and quivering. She stumbled backwards just as they rained down again – this time on and around the table. Nine plucked the spikes from the book and tossed them on the floor.

At least I have the book. Probably better to leave quickly before anything—

There was a strange darkening in the room that Nine couldn't quite put her finger on. And that feeling of being watched. It was coming from behind her.

Slowly, Nine turned round to see the innocent-looking starflower bending over her, the huge petals lifting up like a lid on a hinge. Interlocking, spiny teeth opened into wide jaws with a soft, pink mouth inside.

"Knew you were trouble," huffed Nine. She stuffed the book into her satchel, and ran for the door – but the starflower had other plans.

In what felt like less than a second, it had reached its long stem across the room and scooped her up in its strong jaws, clamping down on her tightly.

"Hey!" cried Nine as she wriggled hopelessly in its grip. Thankfully the teeth didn't quite meet in the middle, but she could still feel the jaws closing in, crushing all the air from her lungs. Taking as deep a breath as she could, Nine grabbed a spine-tooth from the plant's bottom jaw in one hand, and a spine-tooth from its top jaw in the other. Her arms shaking, she pushed with all her strength – trying to prise them apart.

"Oh. No. You. Don't!" puffed Nine. With a final push, she yanked the jaws apart, rolled out of the flower's mouth and tumbled back down to the floor with a crash, her satchel flopping on top of her. But the starflower was leaning over her again, jaws opening wider – wider—

Quickly, Nine scrabbled beside her for something to throw. Her hands found the bucket – she shuddered as the orange slime billowed around her fingers – and she hurled the contents at the plant's giant mouth.

She looked up just in time to see the jaws closing, and the starflower coming back into position, standing upright once more, with a strange sound – almost like a sigh of satisfaction. Its petals looked more shimmery and golden, and there was a definite air of smugness about it.

Nine shook her head. She would never understand this House and why everything – absolutely everything – had to cause her so much trouble.

"I'm watching you," Nine said, pointing at the starflower. Wiping the sweat from her forehead, she picked up the now hole-ridden book, gave one last glance at the conservatory and made her way to the door.

CHAPTER 9

Nine stomped her way back to the kitchen. Eric was positioning another bucket underneath the orange gloop slowly dripping from the ceiling. Flabberghast and Spoon looked up as she reached into her satchel and slammed the book on the kitchen table. The sugar bowl wisely hopped backwards.

"The conservatory *nibbles a bit*, does it?" snapped Nine. She slammed both of her hands down upon the cover, leaning forwards on the table, and glared at him. "I nearly got stabbed by a cactus!"

"Ah, most unfortunate. It must be moulting season..."

"And that starflower nearly ATE me!"

"It wouldn't have actually swallowed you, Madam. Eric feeds it all the leftover pancakes." He lowered his voice. "Thank goodness someone likes them." He cleared his throat. "The starflower was only being ... playful."

"Playful?! Every room in this House wants to kill me."

"Nonsense, Madam!" scoffed Flabberghast. "The laundry is perfectly harmless." He glanced warily at Nine, slowly sliding *Magical Houses and How to Tame Them* from underneath her palms. He licked his finger and flicked through the pages.

"Plant naughty," said Eric, looking at Nine with his big yellow eyes. "Snatch pancakes." He moved towards her, hesitantly stretching out his huge hand as if to pat her head. "Lady fine?"

"Of course Lady fine," said Nine, dodging his hand. "Lady always fine."

Eric smiled a little sad smile and dropped his arm to his side. He placed a little, stripy boiled sweet on the table and edged it towards Nine with a long fingernail. Nine pushed away the uncomfortable feeling of guilt and blamed the plants for putting her in such a bad mood and hurting his feelings. She picked up the sweet and gave Eric a small smile.

"Hiccups … hiccups…" said Flabberghast, flicking through the book, his eyes darting from page to page.

"Come on, lad!" snapped Spoon.

Flabberghast slammed his finger on the page. "Aha! 'Chapter Twelve: When Your House Has Hiccups'." He turned to the page and skimmed the text. "Causes… Symptoms… How not to lose your chimney… Ah! Curing." He looked up, wide-eyed. "Oh, my stars! Left uncured, house hiccups can last for years!"

"Years?!" said Nine. "I'm not putting up with this for—"

WHOMP! Stomach-twist. Brain-jump.

Everyone was pulled face first onto the floor, drawn by some invisible force. They picked themselves up again.

"—years!" finished Nine.

Flabberghast returned to the book. "Fear not!" he crowed. "Apparently, we just need to give it a drink! Eric, pour water down the sink. Spoon, try the drainpipes. Madam, go to the bathroom behind the shell door. Turn the taps on as fast as you can. And if you can catch the toilet, give it a flush for good measure."

Nine sighed. The toilet. Although most of the House had returned to normal – whatever that was – once they had broken the curse, they still could never find the toilet when they needed it.

"So, it's not stuck upside down above your bed any more?" Nine said wearily.

"Sixth floor," said Spoon, as he dashed off, "and watch out, lass. It's started burping."

"Smell bad," Eric whispered.

Nine tutted. "Oh, for goodness—"

WHOMP! Nine rubbed her head. If her brain jumped any more, surely it would leave her head permanently.

Flabberghast peered into the cupboard, then hastily retreated, slammed the door and rested his back against it. His eyes were wide with alarm. Eric began to wring his tail.

Suddenly a stifling wave of heat swept through the kitchen, taking Nine's breath away.

Was that the sound of flames crackling somewhere…?

"Ah. Swift as you can, Madam," squeaked Flabberghast. "The sky appears to be on fire."

"Of course it is!" snapped Nine, as she hurtled down the hallway towards the portrait-lined staircase. Years. She could not live like this for *years*. Why had she ever stepped foot inside this house?

She dashed up the stairs, two at a time, grabbing the banister handrail for support. It became hotter and hotter under her fingers. She looked down and saw faint wisps of smoke drifting up from the banister. Heat was closing in on her, everywhere. She glanced up dizzily at the witchy portrait she stood beside: Millicent the Goat-Eater (1410–1672). The painting began to melt, the colours blurring, slipping out of shape – until just Millicent's eyes remained, wide in horror, in the middle.

Nine swallowed hard and wiped the sweat from her forehead. She pushed on until she reached the landing, scanning for a shell door. There! Up a ladder – a blue door with a circle of cockleshells on it, which were rearranging themselves in different patterns every couple of seconds. She staggered to the ladder and began to climb. Wisps of smoke curled up out of the rungs.

The hot metal handle stung her hand as she opened the door. A huge, circular bath filled the room. Tufts of brown fur were scattered everywhere, and big, muddy footprints decorated the floor, walls and – rather curiously – the ceiling. Nine scrambled into the bath, her dry throat longing for the sound ... feel ... taste ... of glorious water. It wasn't just the House that needed a drink.

She reached for the brass taps, struggling, twisting... *Good grief!* It must have been Eric's strong hands that had closed them last.

Finally, water, glorious water, cascaded down. Nine flopped underneath it for a moment, mouth open to snatch the precious liquid. Then she reached for the other tap and twisted it as far as she could. Anything – *anything* – to stop those awful hiccups.

Nine sank her hands down underneath the taps, letting the cool water run over her fingers as it fell to the plughole.

Just give it a moment... Had it worked? Were they gone? Yes! It looked like the hiccups had finally—

WHOMP! Stomach-twist. Brain-jump. Heat gone. And a powerful, irresistible force pulled on her fingers. No time to think. To move. To scream. Because she was being pulled, arm first, down the plughole.

CHAPTER 10

Down she plunged into watery darkness, hurtling through a black, swooshing, whooshing tunnel faster than her brain could process it. Nine cried out as the tunnel turned sharply to the right, and her outstretched arms banged into hard metal before she was pulled further down. Her satchel thumped around her, the music box tinkling.

Everything was black … wet … fast…

CRASH! Nine had landed in a watery heap inside a very small space. She put her hand above her head – there was some kind of hatch. She pushed it open and pulled herself up.

Nine looked around and glowered: her head was poking out of the white toilet on the woodenfloorboarded hallway of what was presumably the sixth floor.

"What the...?"

She pushed herself out and stared in disbelief. Not only had she climbed out of a toilet, but somehow her clothes were dry, if slightly smelling of—

The toilet belched. Nine gagged as the toxic fumes billowed around her. Who or *what* had been in here, she didn't even want to imagine...

She leapt for the chain, her hand outstretched – but the toilet suddenly jumped backwards, out of reach, and Nine hit the floorboards face first.

"Oi!" Nine yelled, her arm still scrabbling for the flush. But the toilet giggled mischievously and hopped away on its pedestal. "I hate toilets!" Nine called after it.

She paused for a moment to look at the sixth floor. She had never ventured this high before. There were still endless doors of all shapes and sizes, and the spiral staircase snaked its way up, like a curved spine, to that unreachable, ornately painted ceiling. The House might have eleven storeys on the outside, but there were definitely more inside. She stared at the staircase and put her hand on the rope handrail which spiralled up alongside the stairs...

Where does it go? What's up there? There was so much still to explore...

"Madam, if you can hear me," called out Flabberghast from somewhere downstairs, "the drink didn't work. But fear not. Just hold on to something. Grimlock the Indomitable had another marvellous idea!"

Panic flashed through Nine. She dropped the handrail, dashed for the hallway stairs and hurtled down.

Oh, good grief, no.

She had nearly reached the bottom.

Not a marvellous idea. Anything but a marvellous—

WHOOSH! Suddenly Nine felt herself jolted upside down. She screamed as she clung to the banister railings with both of her hands, her legs dangling in the air. She looked around, wordlessly.

No. Nine wasn't upside down. The *House* was. Nine tumbled to the hallway ceiling, staring in amazement at all the furniture which hadn't moved, but stayed fitted to the floor ... but the floor had become the ceiling. From what was now probably the kitchen ceiling, a probably-upside-down hat stand whistled cheerily.

"WHAT NOW?" bellowed Nine.

Spoon hurtled into view at the bottom of the stairs. Or was it the top? "The lad's tried turning the blasted House upside down."

"Yes, I gathered that!" said Nine, wondering how exactly she was going to climb up – or down – the stairs to get to the bottom – or was it the top?

"And why on earth is the trophy cabinet and everything still stuck to the carpet?"

The Spoon raised a bushy eyebrow. "You've not landed in this House before, have you, lass? Everything *needs* to be stuck to the carpet."

Nine let go of the banister and dropped to the hallway ceiling.

WHOOSH! The House turned round the right way again, and Nine and Spoon tumbled to the plum carpet in the hallway, landing at the foot of the stairs.

"Will you stop doing that?!" cried Nine, as Flabberghast burst out of his study door, in a stumbling, fumbling blur of indigo.

"Clearly, nothing is working," he said weakly, still holding *Magical Houses and How to Tame Them*.

"Clearly!" said Spoon and Nine, both glaring at the wizard.

"But fear not, for Grimlock the Indomitable—"

"Really? *More* marvellous ideas?" said Nine.

"The book suggests giving the House a fright."

"I'll give YOU a fright," grumbled Spoon.

"Aaaaaand," continued the wizard in an over-loud voice, "I've consulted my maps. According to my calculations, there's a world coming up which has a rather … unfavourable reputation." Flabberghast cleared his throat. "If I can land the House there, it might just do the trick."

"What kind of unfavourable reputation?" said Nine, folding her arms.

Flabberghast squirmed a little. "It is not exactly welcoming to visitors."

"Great," said Nine, throwing her hands up in the air. "Perfect. This can only end well."

"As long as we stay in the House, Madam, we will be perfectly safe. Now," he continued, "the House hasn't landed for three years, and I'm not entirely sure it will be very happy about it, especially with a nasty bout of—"

WHOMP! A large puff of pink smoke stood where Flabberghast had once been.

Nine and Spoon looked at each other, then at the puff of pink smoke as it faded into nothing.

"Definitely an improvement," muttered Spoon.

"Oh, out of the way!" said Flabberghast from the staircase behind them. He barged between Nine and Spoon, straightening his hat…

Then he stopped.

Because there was a rumbling. A sickening, unsettling rumbling, getting steadily louder. The trophies in the trophy cabinet rattled and chinked.

"Um," Flabberghast squeaked, "I do believe the House is getting a little bit cross now."

"Oh, really?" said Nine, with her hands on her hips. "Can't think why! You've only flooded it and turned it upside down while flying it through the MOST PERILOUS PLACE in the universe when it's NOT EVEN FLOWN FOR THREE YEARS. And now you're about to land it somewhere with an UNFAVOURABLE REPUTATION to SCARE THE LIVING DAYLIGHTS OUT OF IT!

Really, Flabberghast? Is it *really* getting a little bit cross now?"

Flabberghast twisted his mouth doubtfully, then pointed a finger up in the air and waggled it. "We shall persevere. Brace yourselves!" He darted into his study as Nine sighed loudly. For a brief moment, she could guess how Mr Downes had felt...

Flabberghast slammed the study door. Nine watched as it melted away, leaving in its place a black oblong, speckled with a multitude of sparkling dots, connected by slowly twisting silvery lines.

"Is that a map?" breathed Nine, staring in amazement. "Are these all worlds?"

"Never mind that now," said Spoon. "You think hopping in and out of the worlds is bad? Wait until the House actually lands! Good luck, lass." Then he sprinted off towards the kitchen. The House began shuddering and juddering. Nine sat down on the bottom stair and clung to the banister post.

"Lady? LADY?" came a desperate troll voice. Eric lolloped up the hallway, lurching left and right as the House shook violently. "Lady!" a look of relief briefly came over his face. "House land!" whimpered Eric. "Not like."

Nine tried to reply, but she couldn't. There was a strange feeling, like her brain was being sucked down through her body and out through her feet. She felt sick and dizzy. Everything was moving too fast, hurtling in a direction she didn't understand, but which was quite possibly "down", at a ridiculously fast pace. Her eyes couldn't focus. She felt Eric's rough and bark-like arms wrap around her like a shield.

There was whispering from her satchel – secret words from her precious music box – then…

THUD! Nine's teeth rattled inside her head and her bones jiggled inside her body. She lost her grip on the end of the banister and she and Eric tumbled onto the hallway carpet.

Suddenly, the front door flew open. There was a deafening roar as the most forceful, enraged gusts of wind came from everywhere. Flabberghast's study door burst open, slamming against the wall. The wind swept him out of his study, sending him floating and flailing towards the front door.

It whooshed down the stairs, carrying a thrashing, sword-waving spoon who was trying desperately to keep his kilt in place.

The wind hit Nine and Eric, sweeping them up like leaves in a hurricane.

Nine couldn't breathe – couldn't move…

"Cloak!" wailed Flabberghast, as he tumbled in the air, almost at the front door. He stretched out his hand towards the umbrella stand. A bright blue arm shot up out of the stand, holding an indigo, star-speckled cloak aloft. Flabberghast snatched it as he passed, then out of the door they all hurtled, landing outside in a floppy tumble of wizard, cloak, troll, duster, spoon, kilt, girl and satchel.

Nine looked up at the House. Right in their faces, the front door slammed decisively.

And all was silent.

CHAPTER 11

"**D**id the House just throw us out?" said Nine indignantly, extracting herself from underneath Flabberghast's elbow. They all staggered to their feet. "And there has *got* to be a better way to land that thing."

"Nonsense, Madam," said the wizard, staggering to his slippered feet. "It was perfectly fine."

He wobbled and face-planted onto the floor.

"Never mind that," said Spoon grimly. "Look!"

They were in the greyest, bleakest place that Nine had ever seen – including the dark, repulsive pickpocket den she'd spent most of her life in. At least there had been splashes of colour from their stolen prizes. Here, the sandy soil they stood on was a soft, pale grey, like faded ash. The swathe of forest near by was slate-grey, the sky was dark grey as if all other colours in the world had been sucked away…

But it was what Nine heard that sent a shiver down her spine. A strange faint wheezing on the breeze.

"You fool of a wizard!" growled Spoon. "First you bring us to this land of doom, then you get us trapped outside in it!"

" 'As long as we stay in the House, Madam, we will be perfectly safe,' " quoted Nine.

"Well!" flustered Flabberghast. "The House is unpredictable! That's one of its … charms."

Nine, Flabberghast, Eric and Spoon all shifted closer together, staring at the bleak wood.

"I'm sure the House truly wishes us no harm and will let us in," said Flabberghast, inching backwards and reaching for the front door handle. "It's just a little perplexed." He gritted his teeth, gazing up at its towering front. "Poor, *dear* thing." He turned the door handle.

It was locked.

Flabberghast rattled the door handle helplessly. "Gahhh! Wretched, intolerable building!"

WHOMP! Nine watched in amazement as the House left the ground temporarily as it hiccupped – and crashed back down again. A wave of barely visible magic rolled out from the House, knocking Flabberghast back onto his bottom. He shook his fist at the House. "First I'm locked *inside* my House for three years, and now I'm locked out!"

"At least it's not world-jumping now it's landed," said Nine. "There must be some way to get inside."

"Madam, clearly you have never tried to get inside a magical house which doesn't want you to. It can be intolerably stubborn."

"Sounds familiar," said Nine, glaring at Flabberghast.

WHOMP! They all wobbled at the wave of magic. A roof tile fell off and smashed at their feet. Nine heard a tiny voice whispering inside her satchel.

Suddenly, terrifying high-pitched screeches echoed in the grey trees, followed by the same strange wheezing sound. Nine balled her hands into fists.

Out of the forest stepped a pack of about twenty strange rainbow-coloured creatures, a little shorter than Nine. They looked like they could walk upright, but instead scrambled on their four long, ungainly legs. Their heads were round but – Nine shuddered – their faces were mostly taken up with what looked like a huge, round gaping mouth.

"What… What are those?" said Nine, a jolt of panic rushing through her.

"Trouble," said Spoon solemnly, unsheathing his sword and turning towards the creatures.

The pack began stomping on the ground. As one, Nine, Flabberghast, Eric and Spoon all walked backwards, until their backs bumped the front door of the House.

"If you want to make your fingertips all sparkly and shoot some magic out, now would be a good time," said Nine, not taking her eyes off the rainbow creatures.

"Yes," said Flabberghast. He cleared his throat and shuffled on the spot. He held his fingers in front of him, and silver sparkles danced at his fingertips.

"DO something!"

"I AM TRYING, MADAM!" He thrust his fingers out but nothing happened.

"Turnip! Turnip!" pleaded Eric, pointing to the creatures.

The silver sparkle at Flabberghast's fingertips fizzled and died.

"Is that it?" said Nine, whirling round to Flabberghast.

"I've been without my magic for three years! I'm just a bit rusty!"

"A BIT RUSTY?!"

"I knew it!" roared Spoon. "You are the worst wizard in the world!"

The rainbow creatures edged forwards, stomping as they came. Flabberghast reached behind him, shook the handle and pounded on the door. "Let us in!"

WHOMP! They were all jolted forwards a few steps by the invisible force of the hiccups, then quickly retreated to the walls of the House. And then the wheezing started. The unnerving high-pitched sound was coming from the creatures' wide-open toothless mouths, as if they were sucking in air. But it wasn't air they were taking.

Nine gasped and pointed at Spoon's kilt. "Your pink ribbons! They're sucking the pink away!" They watched in horror as the colour seemed to be pulled away from one of the ribbons, towards the creatures, leaving grey in its place. The little band of pink slapped onto – or was it into? – one of the creatures, which now bore a stripe of pink on its mismatched rainbow body.

"You foul fiends! I'll have your flamin' heads!" Spoon lunged forwards, waving his sword furiously, but Nine grabbed him and held him aloft, his arms and legs swishing wildly in mid-air.

"Gahhh!" cried Flabberghast.

Nine turned and saw the indigo being stretched and pulled away from his pyjamas.

"We're about to have the colour sucked out of us!"

"I fear it's worse than that, Madam." Flabberghast gulped and pointed at the creatures. "Look!"

Nine looked. And wished she hadn't.

She dropped Spoon in horror as she saw, one by one, circular rows of jagged teeth pop up inside the creatures' huge mouths. They stomped and wheezed and edged ever closer. Nine saw the brown of her satchel being sucked towards the creatures.

"Get your mouths off me!" she yelled, pulling her satchel backwards. Inside, the little music box tinkled.

WHOMP! The House's burst of magic whomped them a step closer to danger.

The creatures approached the House with interest. The inhaling noise came again and the blue began lifting away from the door.

"There! See!" Flabberghast yelled at the House, wildly waving his arms. "They're coming to get you! *Now* you can be frightened! *Now* you can stop those infernal hiccups!"

There was a moment of silence.

WHOMP! "Aaaargh!" wailed Flabberghast, clutching handfuls of curly hair which poked out from beneath his hat.

"How can this place not scare the hiccups out of the flamin' House?" said Spoon.

"It's scaring the living daylights out of *me*," said Nine. "We need to get inside NOW."

"And how do you propose we do that, Madam?!"

"Back door?" said Nine.

"Locked!"

"Smash a window?"

"Utterly shatterproof. I replaced them after the incident with the green-horned minotaurs."

Spoon unsheathed his sword. "I wish I could replace YOU! I tell you, if I had an ounce of magic in my body, I'd turn YOU into a turnip."

"No turnip! No turnip!" Eric cried.

"No one is turning ANYONE into a vegetable!" said Nine. "Just let me think. We need a plan!"

"I have a plan!" bellowed Spoon. "YAAA-AAAAHHHHH!" He raised his sword and charged at the surprised rainbow creatures.

Eric whimpered as Spoon leapt and clambered over the creatures' backs, whilst they batted at him, as if he were an annoying, kilt-wearing fly.

"I'll teach you to steal the pink from my kilt, you miserable beasts!"

Nine hesitated – torn between wanting to help Spoon and finding a way into the House.

"AAAAARRRRGHHHH!" wailed Spoon as he lay on his back, being passed along from one creature to the next. The wheezing, inhaling sound came again. The pink from another ribbon on Spoon's kilt disappeared. So did the silver from his sword, leaving it dull and grey.

"My sword! You'll pay for that!" roared Spoon as one of the rainbow creatures tossed him up in the air.

Nine ran around the left-hand side of the House. A shot of hope lit her up inside. "There's a little window open!"

"The one we could never close!" yelled back Flabberghast.

"I could fit through!"

"Then make haste, Madam!" came Flabberghast's voice. "Argh! Leave my hat alone!"

Heart thumping, Nine climbed up onto a window sill. But the open window was still another floor up... Then she peered closely at the wall. Certain bricks jutted out a little further than the others. Footholds. Handholds. All the way up to the open window. Like someone had already thought of doing this...

Nine took a deep breath and carefully began to scale the wall – reaching up, grabbing a brick, moving her legs up on the footholds until, finally, she reached the window. She pushed it further open, tumbled inside – and landed on a soft bed.

From the moment she entered the room, Nine felt a strange sense of peace. A sense, for the first time, that maybe she was right where she should be. Every wall was painted a bold turquoise, and each had a narrow bookcase filled with books. Empty picture frames hung on the walls. There was a golden clock on the shelf, which had stopped...

Time was standing still.

Something like a blue ball of wool on legs scurried away under the bed. There was a brown fabric-bound book lying on the pillow. It looked familiar... Nine reached over, lifted the book and read the golden letters on the spine. *The Mystery of Wolven Moor.* She opened the book and saw a name handwritten inside: Eliza.

Nine frowned. There were secrets here. Nine could feel them stirring, whispering into her head in a voice that didn't exist. She yearned to explore – to embrace – every inch of the room.

And even more strange was the *smell* of the room. It was familiar. Like something she had smelled before but couldn't quite put her finger on.

"GAHHH!" came Spoon's voice from outside.

His voice snapped Nine from her thoughts. She pushed away the strange lure of the room and ran to the bedroom door. She flung it open, hurtled down a rickety flight of stairs and headed to the plum-carpeted staircase. She half-ran, half-fell down the stairs and threw herself at the front door, yanking it open with trembling fingers.

"Lady save!" cried Eric, lolloping towards the door.

Flabberghast leapt for the door at the same time, and for one ridiculous moment, he and Eric were wedged in the doorframe together, unable to move. Nine reached forwards and heaved on Eric's thick arms, pulling them free.

"Come *on*, Dr Spoon!" cried Flabberghast, turning to Spoon, who sat astride one of the creatures, sword held aloft. "Cease fooling around!"

As Spoon leapt off the creature and rolled across the grey ground, Nine saw all the ribbons on his precious kilt had been un-pinked. He darted inside the House and Nine slammed the front door.

Punch. Slam. Thump. The door was pummelled by the furious creatures, wheezing and screeching.

"Time to go," she said.

"Indeed, Madam," said Flabberghast breathlessly, as Nine pulled the toad's tongue on the coat of arms.

ZA-BAM! There was a sickening lurch, followed by the strange – yet now familiar – feeling that her brain was being sucked out of the top of her skull. She tried to gasp air that didn't exist. Everything hurtled in a direction she didn't understand but was quite possibly "up". Then there was a strange lightness as the House jolted back into the World Between Worlds.

CHAPTER 12

"**I** do not know how to cure these hiccups," said Flabberghast, leaning against the front door. "I have no choice but to use my question for the Tower at the End of Time. We shall go to the Championship, and hope I make it that far."

WHOMP!

It began to pour with rain inside the House. Nine yelped and put her arms over her head as freezing drops trickled down the back of her neck.

Eric whimpered and grabbed a handful of Flabberghast's cloak and tried to pull it over Nine and himself. Flabberghast snatched his cloak back from the troll. He glared at Spoon, then looked at Nine.

"You better had," said Nine, "because I'd rather eat a plateful of Eric's pancakes than put up with this for a minute more!"

"Eric pancake?"

Nine refused to look at Eric and instead stared furiously at the wizard, as if everything was his fault. Which, in all likelihood, it was. The floor beneath them began to shake. And an unsettling feeling of pressure – an intangible, unbearable, air-tingling pressure – began to build up.

Spoon pointed his unsilvered sword all around. "What now?"

The portraits in the hallway and on the staircase began quivering...

The crockery in the kitchen clattered. The trophies in the trophy cabinet rattled ... louder ... louder...

Spoon raised a bushy eyebrow. "I hate to tell you this, lad," he said, "but I think your House is about to explode."

"House boom?" gasped Eric. He grabbed his tail.

"Ohhhh dear," said Flabberghast breathlessly.

SMASH! A plate from the kitchen dresser hit the flagstones.

"I have a nasty suspicion that the House is trying to cure the hiccups itself ... by holding its breath."

"Holding its breath?" asked Nine, hardly believing her ears.

"Yes, Madam, holding its breath!" And Flabberghast stormed off down the hallway towards his study. "It means our time is running perilously short. So if you'll excuse me, I am going to attempt to steer the House towards Tuesday. We must be nearly there!"

The study door slammed shut in Nine's face and faded away, leaving swirling, dark, angry clouds with occasional flashes of lightning. Nine glared at the no-longer-a-door. The House shook more vigorously.

"My equipment!" said Spoon and dashed upstairs.

SMASH! Another plate hit the kitchen floor.

"Save teapot!" Eric said, hurrying down the hallway. He paused as he reached Nine. "Eric pancake?" he said quietly, then hurried on. Nine stood alone in the pouring rain in the most ridiculous House she had ever known. She huffed in frustration. Frustration that trolls had feelings and she had trampled all over them. Frustration that the pancakes were so awful in the first place. Frustration that wizards were so unreasonably unreasonable.

WHOMP! The House veered sideways. Or was it everyways? Nine closed her eyes, her head spinning, desperately wanting this to end. Stomach-twist. Brain-jump.

And breathe.

CRASH! There was a loud skeleton-falling-out-of-the-wardrobe kind of noise upstairs.

Oh, no! Bonehead!

Nine staggered up the stairs, up the ladder to her bedroom and flung open her door. The wardrobe door was wide open and in front of it on the floor was a jumbled mess of skeleton, his bones all higgledy-piggledy and rattling with the vibrations of the House. She dashed over to Bonehead, catching the skull as it rolled towards her.

"Oh, for goodness' sake!" Nine said, putting

down the skull and picking up random bones to try and work out what went where. "This ridiculous House! It's holding its breath! Everything is falling over. You can't feel it, Bonehead, but the air is tingling and—"

"Actually," said the skeleton, "I feel it. It makes me feel rather … alive."

There was a strange, quick pull in the air, as if magic was being rapidly sucked in by the skeleton from every corner of the room. Nine stared in amazement as all of Bonehead's bones, including the ones now snatched out of her hands, speedily started to connect to each other on the floor, all forming a perfect skeleton, except...

"Er, your hands and your feet are in the wrong place," Nine said.

"Ah," said the skeleton, as the hands and feet quickly rearranged themselves.

"How did you do that?" said Nine.

"You know, I'm not entirely sure," said Bonehead. "I was a very powerful wizard when I was alive. Of course, no one cares about that when you're dead. They just hide you in a wardrobe and forget you exist."

Judging by the amount of moaning and groaning that had come from the wardrobe since she'd arrived in the House, Nine thought it was unlikely that anyone could ever forget Bonehead existed. She frowned at the wardrobe.

"Bonehead," she said slowly. "Why *are* you a skeleton? How did you … die?"

With a skin-crawling creaking sound, the skeleton turned his skull to face her. "Hopscotch Championship 1831," he said gloomily.

Nine said nothing. Her brain was whirring. The skeleton non-stared at her for a moment with non-eyes, then his skull creaked back to face the window.

DIED in the Hopscotch Championship…

"And … why were you in Flabberghast's wardrobe?"

"You can ask the boy that one," said the skeleton curtly. "Put me in that chair, would you?"

Nine dragged the chair from her desk over to face the window. She scooped up the skeleton, plonked him down and rearranged him to what she hoped was a comfortable position … if skeletons could feel comfortable. He sat there rattling as the House shook around them.

"Watch out. We're landing soon."

"You'll be off somewhere exciting, I expect," said the skeleton gloomily. "While I sit here gathering dust."

"Actually, the Hopscotch Championship," she said, keenly watching his skull for some reaction – then realising that it was utterly pointless. "Flabberghast is going to ask the Tower how to stop the hiccups."

"If he gets that far," droned Bonehead, "which is unlikely. I've seen him in action, you know?"

"Well, he'd better get that far! Because if we don't cure these hiccups and stop the House from holding its breath, it'll probably explode and there'll be no House left!"

No House left... As she said those words, the thought filled Nine with a deep sadness. Yes, she did feel unsure she had made the right decision. Yes, it felt like the family she yearned for was falling apart. But there was so much she still wanted to know about the House – so much she wanted to know about everything... She thought of her music box. How utterly ridiculous had her life become that she was here, even thinking of trusting a skeleton with her secrets? And yet...

"My music box is whispering," Nine said, taking her music box out of her satchel.

The skeleton seemed to peer closer. "Oh. Now where did you get that from?"

"I've had it since I was small. I'd been left in a doorway. Probably a workhouse or something. Just me and that music box." Nine bit her lip. "If it has something to say, Bonehead, I want to hear it. I wish I could find a way to get into the Tower and ask my question."

"Ooh, you don't want to go there. Most of those who enter the Tower never come out." He reached forwards suddenly, with surprising speed, and his fleshless fingers grasped her hand. She gasped. "When they enter, they must choose their answer wisely," he said, in a melancholy voice. "And I didn't."

"Choose *their* answer?" Nine frowned. "What do you mean?"

"Brace yourselves!" came Flabberghast's voice from downstairs. "We're landing!"

The skeleton released its grip and turned to

look out of the window. "Ooh, here we go," he said, sounding rather excited.

Nine didn't reply. She staggered over and clung to the iron frame of her bed. Her brain was being sucked down through her feet... She gasped vanishing air...

THUD! There was air once more.

"Much better when you don't have a brain. Landing tickles the skull rather pleasantly now."

"Lucky you," said Nine, as she staggered to her feet.

She looked out of the bedroom window and gasped. Everywhere she looked, there was an explosion of colour – flags, bunting and banners saying HOPSCOTCH CHAMPIONSHIP 1838. Hundreds of wizards and witches were milling around, or floating through the air, cloaks of every shade and pattern trailing behind them.

"Madam!" called a frustrated wizard from downstairs. "Make haste!"

Nine stood at the door. "Keep an eye – well, an eye socket – on the House for us. Don't let it get stuck in a different world. Or explode. Or do anything ridiculous."

If skulls could raise eyebrows, Nine would have sworn Bonehead raised one.

"Well, anything *more* ridiculous than it already is."

And she walked out, shutting the vibrating bedroom door behind her.

CHAPTER 13

The portraits swung wildly as she ran down to the front door. The tingling in the air made the hairs on the back of her neck stand up. She was about to set foot in another world, and one full of wizards, witches, magic – and hopscotch.

Eric, Spoon and Flabberghast stood in the hall, the wizard wearing his indigo hat and star-speckled indigo cloak. He opened the front door and they were greeted by a wave of deafening noise – laughing, talking, cheering, a brass band and occasional explosions.

Flabberghast took a deep breath, held his head high and marched out, Spoon trotting beside him. Eric stood in the doorway, looking at the door, clutching his feather duster and wringing his tail.

"Oh, for goodness' sake," muttered Nine, as she came up behind him. She nudged Eric outside and shut the front door behind her. "You're safer out here than you are in the House!"

She turned to look back up at her home. The windows were rattling as the House held its breath. Nine wondered how long it could last. Another roof tile fell off and landed by Nine's feet, and the chimney pot wobbled dangerously from side to side. Bonehead stared out of the window with lifeless eyes and waved stiffly to her. Nine gave a little wave back. Perfectly normal waving to a skeleton in your bedroom. Perfectly. Normal.

"I finish the hopscotch. I make it to the Tower. I ask my question. We save the House," Flabberghast muttered to himself.

Nine looked him up and down. "Perfect. What could possibly go wrong? Just one question... Why on earth are you still wearing your slippers?"

Flabberghast looked down and grimaced. "Ah." He turned around quickly. "I'll just—"

The front door shut itself, and there was a smug-sounding locking noise.

"Never mind," Flabberghast sang through gritted teeth. "Welcome to Tuesday."

A middle-aged witch in a puffy crinoline dress and velvet cloak glided past effortlessly. She looked at the vibrating house, at Eric with his duster and at Flabberghast with his slippers. Flabberghast gave her a very fake grin. "Morning."

She snorted in disgust and flew on.

Flabberghast grabbed Eric's duster and stuffed it in the letterbox mounted on the outside of the House. "Leave it there," he hissed. "Or they'll laugh at you."

"Can you do that?" Nine asked, watching the gliding witch. "Can you fly, too?"

"Flying is highly overrated," said Flabberghast.

A huge red urn about half the size of the front door hovered in the air above them. The urn was decorated randomly with golden numbers from one to ten. As Nine watched it float around, the lid rose up above the urn and the familiar voice of the message witch droned out.

"TEN MINUTES UNTIL THE CHAMPION-SHIP BEGINS... THE CHAMPIONSHIP BEGINS IN TEN MINUTES."

The red urn floated on, repeating its message.

"Marvellous," murmured Flabberghast, with all the enthusiasm of a squashed frog. "Just in time."

A swoosh of witches and wizards swept past in the air. Excited chattering came from everywhere.

Flabberghast led them towards a large crowd. A square arena was marked out in bunting, each triangle displaying a single number. At the far end stood a raised platform, on which there were three wooden chairs and a long table with a huge scroll on it. A short distance in front of it was a long golden line with flagpoles bearing hopscotch grid flags at either end.

The place was colourful, chaotic and unlike anything Nine had ever seen. The closest she could think of was the hustling, bustling street market where she used to pickpocket before she joined the House. But the cobbled stones, buildings and stalls seemed dull in comparison to this.

Then a strange and terrible and curious thought pricked at her mind... The last time she had pickpocketed a witch, she had ended up with the miniature House, which had popped up to become the home she now lived in. How about the witches and wizards here? What amazing things did they have in their pockets? All the pushing and shoving... Surely they wouldn't notice the swift fingers of a clever thief.

Nine pushed the thought away as they stopped at the fringe of the crowd. "Where's the Tower?"

"You find it when you complete the hopscotch," said Flabberghast. "I have been a couple of times before. Once in 1831, which did *not* go to plan, and once in 1835 which did – the year I was champion and Gazillion was..." He looked around shiftily.

"A turnip, for some unknown reason," finished Nine sharply. She saw a kiosk with a long queue of impatient-looking witches and wizards, twisting their necks towards the throng of swooshing witches and wizards. "What are they doing?"

"Queuing for magice," said Flabberghast.

"Magice? What's magice?"

"Magic – and ice, Madam," Flabberghast snapped. He pulled his indigo hat lower over his face and dipped his head.

Nine's eyes widened. She watched as a witch

walked away from the kiosk with a lilac cone in her hand. On top of the cone was a little blue flickering flame. The witch held out her hand, and golden sparks shot from her fingertips into the flame. For a moment, the flame expanded and exploded, then in its place were piled two round scoops of green ice cream. The witch licked it and merged into the crowd.

"I'm not sure about *eating* magic," said Nine, wrinkling her nose. A witch floated by holding a stick with what looked like sky-blue candyfloss, except it was fizzing and sparkling. "Well, what about that?"

"Best not. Fizzlefloss is bad for your teeth, Madam," said Flabberghast, looking over his shoulder. "And your elbows."

"Your elbows?" Nine's stomach rumbled. "Well, what *can* I eat?"

A young pink-haired wizard floated by holding a tray with rows of identical-looking doughnuts. Flabberghast waved him down, handed over some coins and took four doughnuts.

"A doughnut?" Nine said, examining hers. "What's inside?"

"A Don't-Know-Nut," corrected Flabberghast, looking shiftily around. "And it's a surprise."

"Oh, good," growled Spoon.

Eric gulped down the doughnut in one go. He went pale and shivery, then red and sweaty, then returned to normal.

"An Ice 'n' Spice," said Flabberghast.

Spoon nibbled his doughnut suspiciously, then started floating up into the air. Flabberghast grabbed his leg and pulled him back down, as Spoon desperately tried to hold his kilt close. "An Extra Light."

Nine took a bite of the soft, doughy outside, then felt something small and weird jumping around inside her mouth. She froze for a moment, then spat it out. Something like a red berry with legs and a snapping mouth scuttled away, snarling.

"Jawberry Scram," said Flabberghast, as Nine cautiously finished the now-safe doughnut. "Bad luck, Madam." He bit into his doughnut and a gush of green goo squirted up into his face.

A group of witches and wizards floated by and gave Flabberghast a disapproving look.

"Morning," he muttered, smiling through the goo.

"Pathetic," muttered one of the witches.

"Oh," said another. "Wasn't he involved in that Dreadful Incident in 1831?"

Flabberghast's smile dropped as they floated on. He looked nervous. "Listen, Madam, I'm beginning to think coming here was a mistake," he said in a low voice. His eyes were wide and pleading.

"You need the answer from the Tower," said Nine, frowning. "And I thought hopscotch meant everything to you!"

"Yes. Well. Now that I'm here…" He swallowed hard. "I know we need to cure the House's hiccups. There must be another way."

WHOMP! There was a strange whoosh of energy behind them. Nine and the others spun around and stared.

"The House has disappeared!" squeaked Flabberghast.

"Aye, and it's a pity you weren't inside when it did! Fool!" said Spoon, hopping up onto Nine's shoulder.

"Better a fool than a failure!" said Flabberghast.

WHOMP! The House reappeared, still vibrating. One window was smashed, and the roof was dripping in sickly olive-coloured slime. Nine glanced up at her bedroom window. Bonehead raised a bony thumbs up.

Nine turned back to see Flabberghast standing frozen to the spot. He had turned paler than his china teacups and his eyes were fixed on a hooded figure descending from the skies. The figure landed beside them in a swirl of emerald cloak. And as a hand with green painted nails emerged from under the cloak's folds, Flabberghast could only make a high-pitched, strangled squeak:

"Ah."

CHAPTER 14

The figure barged between Nine and Flabberghast, causing Nine to stumble backward, and patted Flabberghast's cheek. "Flabberghast the Unworthy!" said a rich voice, sounding like it was laced with spikes. The figure lowered her hood, revealing a thick, wild spring of curly white hair. "Well, well. We haven't seen your face in years. How the devil are you?"

Flabberghast opened his mouth and closed it again, staring at the witch wide-eyed.

Nine pushed in beside Flabberghast and stared at the stranger. She was an older witch, with wrinkles forming frowns rather than smiles, and cold purple eyes.

"He's fine," said Nine. "*Who* the devil are *you*?"

Spoon jumped up onto Nine's shoulder. He drew his sword and pointed it at the witch.

The witch laughed without mirth. "I'm his aunt. Ophidia the Unpredictable. I say, Flabberghast, these are rather endearing creatures. Such well-trained pets." She twisted her hand into a claw-like shape and a crackling green light shot out from her fingertips and gently flicked Spoon from Nine's shoulder.

Spoon landed in a heap of kilt, sword and moustache by Flabberghast's feet. "How dare you!" he roared, leaping to his feet. But Nine clamped one hand over his mouth and the other around his spindly body. Spoon burbled furiously, his limbs thrashing in outrage.

"I heard that your curse was broken, dear. Goodness, look at the dreadful state of your house. Turning red and looking ghastly! Oh, don't say it's got hiccups!"

Flabberghast squirmed. "We're fixing that."

"Yes…" said Ophidia. "I'm not sure houses are meant to have bubbles coming out of their chimneys. One to ask the Tower, perhaps. Should you make it that far."

Ophidia squinted at the House. Nine followed her gaze and could just about make out Bonehead waving at the window. "Oh, my stars!" said Ophidia, pointing at the skeleton. "That's not—"

"No, it absolutely certainly is not," gabbled Flabberghast.

"Aldous the Gloom-Stricken? I haven't seen him since *that* event in 1831." She raised her eyebrows and looked at Flabberghast, who squirmed. "But I'd recognise that gloomy expression, dead or alive!" Her tone was edged with darkness. "Fancy him being in your house."

"Yes, fancy. Well, must dash." Flabberghast moved forwards.

Ophidia's emerald-cloaked arm shot out to stop him. "Marvellous to see you competing, dear. You know, they've finally let the witches join in now! About time."

"Most splendid!" said Flabberghast, nodding enthusiastically.

"Such a shame your sister couldn't make it."

"A pity indeed." Flabberghast tried to push past Ophidia's arm, but it held firm.

"And of course you'll have heard that Gazillion

the Unstoppable has been released from the terrible spell that bound him."

"Couldn't be happier!" said Flabberghast, through gritted teeth. He tried to move forwards again, but stopped suddenly. An expression of pain appeared on his face. Nine looked down – a very high-heeled, sparkly green shoe was pressing down on Flabberghast's slipper. She glared at the witch but said nothing.

Any witch called "the Unpredictable" was probably not one to pick a fight with at the first meeting.

"He's awfully keen to ask the Tower who cursed him," said Ophidia.

"And I wish him every success," said Flabberghast, painfully extracting his slippered foot.

"Of course you do," said Ophidia smoothly. "Send my regards to your sister. Such a clever witch."

Flabberghast rolled his eyes as Ophidia floated into the air.

Nine released Spoon and placed him on the ground.

"You do that again, lass, and I'll bite your fingers off." Spoon scowled, sheathing his sword.

Nine ignored him. "Flabberghast, do we always have to bump into your relatives?"

"Yes, Madam," snapped Flabberghast. "Apparently we do. Now, I must prepare."

He walked off swiftly into the busy crowd, followed by Eric. Spoon hopped up onto the troll's shoulder as they pushed through the gaggle of witches and wizards, Eric's head visible above the rest.

Nine held back.

The hustling, bustling crowd was so different to anything she'd ever experienced, yet strangely familiar: distracted, excited, careless. She thought of her days as a pickpocket in the market. It was a different life ... worlds away ... yet she had to admit that her fingers itched for ripe pockets all the same.

The opportunity was a gift – too much to ignore. Nine's heart thumped. Her hands began to sweat. It had been a while, but...

Three.

Oh, she'd missed this...

Two.

Focus on the prey...

One.

Nine pushed forwards, bumping into a passing wrinkly-faced witch with purple-streaked hair, who was gazing skywards.

A velvet cloak... A flash of fingers... A racing heart... A prize!

Nine's fist closed around the stolen treasure as the witch glared with piercing yellow eyes. "Watch your step," the witch muttered, and moved on.

Nine cautiously looked at her prize. A small red velvet drawstring bag. She opened it and tipped the contents into her shaking hand. Four large, dark brown coins, a tiny corked jar with sapphire-blue smoke swirling inside, and a miniature matching blue skull which stared at her accusingly with unseeing eyes. She quickly tipped everything back into the bag before anybody noticed and stuffed it into her satchel.

She searched for Eric among the crowd... There! Her muscles relaxed a little as she saw the troll's head bobbing from side to side in rhythm with his lolloping walk. As she pushed towards him she could just see Flabberghast's indigo hat weaving in front. But where was—?

Nine jumped as Spoon hopped onto her shoulder. His voice was low and suspicious in her ear. "What have you been up to?"

"Nothing," said Nine, glad he couldn't see the velvet bag she pictured in her mind. But – what if someone else could?

A terrible fear began growing inside her chest. What had she done? She was surrounded by magical eyes...

Eric turned around. "Lady fine?"

"Lady always fine," replied Nine automatically, but she felt sick. She had been unwise to take the velvet bag, and as she thought of Ophidia, she began to think perhaps Flabberghast had been right: coming to the Hopscotch Championship at all was a bad idea. But what choice did they have if they wanted the House's hiccups to be cured?

"ALL PARTICIPANTS TO THE ARENA. TO THE ARENA, ALL PARTICIPANTS," droned the familiar voice as the red urn appeared again.

"You can tell she loves her job," muttered Nine, trying but failing to push the worries away.

A golden whoosh of fireworks exploded in the air in the shape of number tens, met by an excited rumble from the crowd. Hundreds of velvet-cloaked wizards and witches began rushing towards the arena like a swarm of colourful flies descending on a rotten apple. Then golden number nines sparkled in the sky...

"Are you ready?" said Nine.

Then eights...

"For which part?" said Flabberghast.

Sevens...

"Do you mean the part where I'm humiliated in front of everyone because I've not had any decent hopscotch practice for three years?"

Sixes...

"Or the part where Gazillion the Recently Unturnipped finds out who turned him into a vegetable?"

"Flabby safe! Flabby stay!" wailed Eric.

Fives...

"I shall do no such thing," sighed Flabberghast. "I shall endure the hopscotch, confront the Tower, cure the House's hiccups..."

Fours...

"And prove to my aunt, and everyone, that I am worthy." And the wizard in pyjamas lifted his nose in the air, took a deep breath ... and tripped over his cloak, falling flat on his face.

Threes...

Eric picked him up by the collar of his cloak and set him on his feet.

Twos...

"Thank you," Flabberghast said curtly. He hitched up his cloak, and marched towards the arena.

Ones...

CHAPTER 15

"**A**LL CONTESTANTS TAKE YOUR POSITIONS. TAKE YOUR POSITIONS, ALL CONTESTANTS."

Nine saw Flabberghast's indigo hat move forwards and out of sight. All around, people pushed and shoved for a better view of the arena.

"Flabby sad."

"Lad's a fool," Spoon grumbled into Nine's ear. "Of all the wizards in all the realms, I had to choose that one."

"Yes, you did!" Something inside Nine snapped. "Because of all the wizards in all the realms, he was the only one who offered you a lift when you needed it!" Nine thought of her former life … barely surviving as a pickpocket… The

131

House had been there when she needed it. The House and the strange collection of characters who lived in it. And Flabberghast was their only chance to save it. Spoon frowned so hard, his bushy eyebrows met in the middle.

"Come on," said Nine, grabbing Eric's hand. Using her satchel, she bashed her way through the last few layers of jabbering witches and wizards, tugging the heavy troll behind her. The image of a downcast but determined Flabberghast kept flashing in her mind. She would not let him face this important – if bizarre – trial alone. There! There was the indigo hat. She gave a final push, and they broke through.

The pleasant bunting began to vanish, melting into a waist-high barrier of red fire to keep the spectators back from the pitch. On the ground was a large, fiery hopscotch grid, every line spitting golden sparks threateningly into the air.

They had ended up by the number ten. Near by was the raised table with three seats. On one sat an older wizard in a blue cloak, jiggling excitedly on his chair and nervously twisting his long grey beard. In the middle sat the message witch, still staring blankly ahead and clutching the huge scroll. And on the final seat sat Ophidia the Unpredictable. Her eyes connected with Nine's and she smiled slowly.

Nine tore her eyes away.

Flabberghast was making his way down to the other end of the pitch. Lined up in a row was an amber-cloaked witch with elaborately plaited black hair and an expression that could probably kill at ten paces, maybe eight on a good day; Gazillion the Unstoppable with his mane of blond-green hair and an expression of contempt for the world; and joining them was Flabberghast the Unworthy with his indigo pyjamas and an expression that suggested he wished he'd caught up with the toilet before he left the House.

Gazillion smiled a thin, determined smile, and raised one of his feet.

STAMP. STAMP. STAMP. STAMP.

A deathly silence fell on the crowd. The amber-cloaked witch lifted her foot and joined him.

STAMP. STAMP. STAMP. STAMP.

Looking terrified, Flabberghast joined them.

STAMP. STAMP. STAMP. STAMP.

Every witch, every wizard began to stamp.

STAMP. STAMP. STAMP. STAMP.

The echoing sound sent chills down Nine's spine. Eric's hand tightened around hers. Spoon edged closer to her head.

The stamping picked up speed.

STAMP-STAMP-STAMP-STAMP.

STAMPSTAMPSTAMPSTAMP.

Until Ophidia the Unpredictable suddenly jumped from her chair – and the crowd fell motionless. Ophidia threw wide her arms and bellowed, "WE HEAR YOUR CALL! MALINDA THE UNDAUNTED, GAZILLION THE UNSTOPPABLE AND FLABBERGHAST THE UNWORTHY: LET THE CHAMPIONSHIP BEGIN!"

Malinda, Gazillion and Flabberghast sprang into action. They all threw something pebble-like towards the grid. Malinda's landed on the number seven, and Gazillion's and Flabberghast's pebbles both landed on the ten. The golden flames turned to a cold blue and rose higher.

Malinda was the first to hop over the fiery blue line, landing with one foot on the number one.

"Hurry up!" growled Gazillion behind Malinda on the grass.

He glared at Flabberghast. Flabberghast glared back.

The crowd held their breath. Malinda was still balancing on one leg. Then she jumped with both feet, landing astride the blue fire on numbers two and three.

The lines surrounding these numbers suddenly twisted and crackled. Malinda looked down at her feet – watching, waiting. Out of the lines, blue fire twisted and swirled and lengthened, creating a long neck with a dragon head at the end.

Flabberghast and Gazillion glared at each other again, then both hopped onto the number one, barely fitting on. They grasped each other's cloaks, each shoving and wobbling on one leg, trying to push the other off the square.

The blue-fire dragon threw back its head, opened its blue flaming mouth, then plunged down towards Malinda.

With a lightning response, Malinda pointed her fingertips at the dragon's head. Amber threads shot from her fingers and wrapped themselves around the dragon's mouth. As the creature writhed and shook its head, Malinda hopped one-footed onto the four.

A towering jack-in-the-box in a crimson cloak and pointed hat popped out of square number four. It was wearing white gloves and its arms stuck out to each side from underneath the cloak. Its mouth was closed but grinning as it rocked back and forth over Malinda, and she leaned left and right to avoid it, wobbling on one leg. The crowd gasped.

"You know," Nine whispered to Eric and Spoon, "I have a feeling that wizard hopscotch isn't quite what I thought it was." She glanced nervously at Flabberghast.

Still wobbling, Gazillion gave Flabberghast a sneaky grin and shot mauve sparks at Flabberghast's feet, making him stand on one foot. As Flabberghast tried not to wobble outside the grid, Gazillion jumped ahead to numbers two and three, his brown-booted feet astride the blue flames.

"Oh no you don't," said Flabberghast behind Gazillion, grabbing his cloak.

Gazillion roared as the pyjamaed wizard pulled him backwards. He twisted around towards Flabberghast, his fingertips sparkling, but at that moment, the dragon broke the amber cords fastening its mouth. Gazillion whirled back around and shot mauve sparkly threads at the dragon, which wrapped around its eyes like a blindfold.

The jack-in-the-box bobbed backwards and forwards, staring with dark, glassy eyes. Nine gasped as it opened its mouth slowly, revealing sharp, pointed teeth. Wobbling wildly, Malinda shot amber threads from her fingertips towards the jack-in-the-box, missing each time. The blindfolded dragon thrashed its head as Flabberghast and Gazillion wrestled.

Then both hopscotch creatures dived down towards Malinda at the same time. The crowd gasped. The witch screeched as the jack-in-the-box reached her first. She desperately shot amber strands at its mouth, which changed the teeth to bubbles. Malinda kicked furiously, popping each tooth with her boots, but the jack-in-the-box brought forward its white-gloved arms. It grasped Malinda and tossed her outside the grid.

She landed with a thud on the grass. Gazillion and Flabberghast – the latter's head underneath Gazillion's armpit – both froze for a moment.

The crowd gave a riotous round of applause as Malinda lifted herself up to bow to the judges then slumped back down onto the ground. The crimson-cloaked jack-in-the-box kept grinning to itself as it shrunk back into its square.

"Hopscotch bad," said Eric, looking at Nine with worried eyes. "Flabby die?"

"I – I don't know," said Nine and she stared as the dragon's blindfold dissolved into mauve sparks. It reared its head, then came crashing down towards the wizards.

CHAPTER 16

Gazillion released Flabberghast from the headlock, his fingers sparkling mauve as the dragon opened its mouth wide ...

... and Flabberghast took off his left fluffy slipper and shoved it inside the rather surprised dragon's mouth. A murmur of discontent mixed with a few sneering chuckles ran around the crowd.

Gazillion, still standing in front of Flabberghast, stared in surprise. "You really are the worst wizard."

Nine's heart leapt as Flabberghast dropped to his hands and knees and crawled through an outraged Gazillion's legs onto number four.

"Flabby ... cheat?" said Eric uncertainly.

Nine shrugged. "I'll tell you when I've worked out the rules."

"What rules?" muttered Spoon.

Up popped the sinister jack-in-the-box. The crimson-clad figure loomed over Flabberghast, who stayed on his hands and knees, crouching on square number four.

The jack-in-the-box rocked back and forth, getting lower and lower, until Gazillion, waiting for it to rock backwards, leapfrogged over Flabberghast's back, landing confidently on numbers five and six.

"Hey!" said Flabberghast. He scrambled to his feet and followed Gazillion, just as the crimson jack-in-the-box rocked right down on the number four, smashing into a thousand crimson shards, which floated away.

Flabberghast and Gazillion rearranged themselves. Gazillion stood on the right, on number six, and Flabberghast stood – one foot slippered, the other slipperless – on number five. They waited.

Nine held her breath.

The crowd held their breath.

Flabberghast and Gazillion held their breath.

Suddenly, deathly pale arms shot upwards, two out of each of the squares, grabbing the wizards' shins. Gazillion began shooting magic at the hands that held him, and Flabberghast yelled as he turned and twisted, trying to shake his off – but the pale fists were locked tight. A third arm shot up from number five and grabbed Flabberghast's cloak. A fourth arm clamped itself around Flabberghast's throat. A fifth snatched his indigo hat, thrusting its fist inside the pointed peak and spinning it around.

"The lad's doomed," said Spoon.

Flabberghast made a choking noise, his eyes bulging.

"Help … me…" he croaked, looking at Gazillion.

"Never!" said Gazillion, zapping a mauve mitten onto one of the confused-looking hands attacking him. "This is hopscotch, Flabberghast! Every wizard for himself!"

Eric dropped Nine's hand and covered his eyes. The panic in Nine's chest exploded into words. "Come on, Flabberghast!"

Flabberghast's fingers scrabbled desperately at the hand at his throat, finally prising it free. He flung it to one side, but it started swinging back towards him. Flabberghast frantically released the fastener of his cloak, and it dropped, along with the arm holding it, down to the hopscotch square. The throat-grabbing arm was heading right for Flabberghast's throat again.

"Punch it! Punch it!" yelled Nine, as several witches and wizards turned round to stare at her.

Flabberghast swung his fist at the incoming hand and knocked it back down again. It woozily tried, and failed, to rise up again.

"YES!" Nine shouted out, as Eric peeped between his thick fingers.

Flabberghast prised the hand from one of his shins, then gave it a good kick, leaving it lying motionless on the ground.

"Come on, lad!" roared Spoon in Nine's ear.

The judges on the platform looked at each other, confused and frowning.

"Where's his magic?" Gazillion pointed at Flabberghast. "This is cheating!"

"He's right," Nine said, turning to Spoon.

"Where *is* his magic?" She stared at Flabberghast as the penny dropped. "I don't think he's just rusty… I think he's lost his magic altogether!"

"Rules?" said Ophidia from the judges' table. The message witch sighed, unrolled the scroll and began to read.

Two of the white arms on Gazillion's square began slapping each other and trying to steal the mitten. Taking his chance, Gazillion leapt onto the seven – and promptly the square turned to bog-like sludge and he disappeared up to his waist.

"Come on, Flabberghast!" called Nine, as the wizard prised the other hand from his shin and kicked it to the ground. "Yes!"

Eric slowly dropped his hands from his face and gave a wonky, tusky grin.

Flabberghast's hat still spun on the final hand, but Flabberghast ignored it. Instead, he placed his hands on Gazillion's turnip-haired head and leapfrogged over him, landing on the eight and nine.

"Yes!" said Nine, then her face fell. "No!" A huge wall of blue fire whooshed up in front of

143

Flabberghast on the line where the number ten box joined the eight and nine. Flabberghast stood motionless, staring at the flame.

Meanwhile, Gazillion was summoning mauve upright poles from his fingertips and placing them either side of him. Gazillion grabbed the poles and heaved himself out of the sludge. He stepped forwards onto the eight and nine behind Flabberghast – and shoved him towards the flame.

"Oi!" yelled Nine, from the side.

"Flame big," said Eric, wringing his tail. "Flame bad."

"Gazillion bad," said Nine.

Flabberghast shuffled back, almost pushing Gazillion off the squares. Gazillion reached his arms either side of Flabberghast and shot mauve sparkly threads towards the flame wall.

"You shall not succeed, Flabberghast the Unworthy!" he bellowed.

A plate-sized, mauve-fringed hole was burning into the blue flame. Nine could just see the number ten through it on the ground. The final number.

"Come on, Flabberghast!" she yelled. "You're nearly there!"

"I shall discover who turnipped me and have my revenge!" said Gazillion. "The Tower is within my reach, Flabberghast!"

"Get to that Tower, lad!" roared Spoon from Nine's shoulder. "Stop those flamin' hiccups or we're doomed!"

Nine's heart thumped as she watched the two wizards pushing, shoving, elbowing, as the hole in the blue flame grew bigger … bigger … big enough to step through!

Flabberghast clenched his jaw and, with a final push at Gazillion, he threw himself through the hole and tumbled forwards.

But Gazillion grabbed Flabberghast as he leapt, then the two tangled wizards crashed down onto number ten…

And vanished from view.

CHAPTER 17

All that remained of Flabberghast was his cloak grasped in one of the hands, his hat still whizzing round on the end of another arm and his slipper in the dragon's mouth. The dragon spat the slipper out and sank back into the hopscotch grid. A few wizards and witches clapped and most wandered off to the various kiosks to buy magice and fizzlefloss.

Nine stared at the hopscotch grid. "Did he make it?" she said, turning to the others. "To the Tower?"

"If he did, you can bet he won't make it back!" said an older witch with frizzy grey hair. "And I don't fancy his chances if that Gazillion the Unstoppable's gone, too. Ooh, he's a nasty piece of work." Nine watched as she flew off towards Grue's Brews, a kiosk selling glasses of ominously frothy yellow liquid.

Nine turned back to the hopscotch grid. No one was watching now. Not even the judges, who were comparing notes at the head table.

"Thank the stars," Ophidia was saying. Nine's ears pricked up. "Unlike his sister, the boy is a disaster. We all remember that catastrophic Championship of 1831."

Bonehead! What exactly did Flabberghast do?

"Flabby gone," said Eric, staring at number ten. "No magic?" He turned to Nine with his big yellow eyes. "Eric help?"

"Well, I have a question I'd like answering," said Nine.

"Aye, and so do I. It could tell me exactly where Dish is. And I'll wager the useless lad will never get the answer to curing the House without us."

Nine glanced over at the House. It was now rocking violently from side to side, with red flares shooting out of its chimney. She couldn't imagine life without the House. And she couldn't imagine the House without the most ridiculous wizard who lived there. She swallowed away the thought.

"He may be useless, but if he doesn't make it back, who am I going to yell at?" Nine gritted her teeth and ducked under the fiery barrier, ignoring Eric's whimpering and his panicked hands scrabbling after her. Spoon clinging to her ear, she ran onto the pitch, grabbed the slipper and cloak, and snatched the still-spinning hat from the fist, which looked as surprised as a fist could look. Nine gave it a slap for extra measure, and it backed off. As Eric lumbered towards her, Nine passed him Flabberghast's things. She needed something small, something magical to throw on the squares, just as Flabberghast and the other contestants had. Of course! She reached inside her satchel.

"Just you wait there, girl!" huffed the wizard judge.

But Nine had no intention of waiting. Her fingers scrabbled at the stolen purse strings and she pulled out the sapphire-blue skull. She raised her hand in the air, showing the skull, and threw it straight onto the ten.

Nine felt a strange warmth, a strange boldness, as the three of them stood there together.

"Ready when you are, lass," said Spoon in Nine's ear.

Her heart thumping, Nine grabbed Eric's hand and squeezed it tight. Then, as one, they jumped straight onto number ten, as the puzzled voice of a distant witch said, "Why didn't we think of that?"

There was heart-stopping silence.

Then Nine was flying down through suffocating darkness. She couldn't speak, couldn't see and couldn't think. She vaguely felt spindly arms releasing her neck and a long-nailed hand slipping out of her grasp...

THUMP! Her feet hit something solid, and she crashed onto the ground. With relief, Nine saw Eric and Spoon were beside her. Nine looked up dizzily and gasped.

There, surrounded by grass, was a tall tower shaped rather like a wonky stone tree, with a large trunk of dark stone at its core, and several stony branches, each leading to pointy-topped turrets. The tallest turret had a purple-slated roof which looked like a wizard hat plonked on top. It was so high it seemed to tickle the clouds. Nine felt a little shiver run down her spine. The Tower looked so calm, so innocent standing there, just minding its own business... So why did it feel like a smiling, welcoming trap, baited and ready to spring?

Nine got to her feet and took Flabberghast's clothes from Eric. They walked over to the Tower, uneasily. Nine eyed it suspiciously. She didn't know what she was looking out for, but something wasn't right about this place.

As they approached, the wooden front door of the Tower swung open. Inside, Nine could see an empty circular room with stone walls and floor, and a ceiling striped with wooden beams. Through an archway on the left, a stone spiral staircase curled up and out of sight.

Nine could hear something now. It was ... laughing? A strange, terrible, voiceless laugh. But she thought of Flabberghast, the House, the music box and the question she so desperately wanted the answer to. There was no backing out now.

"Well," Nine said, hoping she sounded braver than she felt, "let's find some answers and a wizard." She stepped inside the empty room, with

Eric and Spoon beside her.

The door slammed shut.

And everything went dark.

NO ONE IS WELCOME HERE ANY MORE.
THE ENDLESS QUESTIONS ARE NO LONGER
TOLERATED.

Who are you? Why can't I...?

LEAVE NOW AND I WILL SPARE YOU,
ASKER. CAST YOU OUT, BACK FROM WHENCE
YOU CAME.

*Who's talking...? I can't think. Are you inside my
head?*

I AM THE TIMEMASTER. HERE I CONTROL
TIME AND IF YOU STAY, THE SANDS IN THE
HOURGLASS WILL FALL AND YOUR TIME
WILL END.

Everything's so dark, so heavy...

LEAVE WHILE YOU CAN. YOU DO NOT
WANT TO ASK THE TOWER ANYTHING.

Think. There was a question. Whispering...

YOU DO NOT HAVE A QUESTION FOR
THE TOWER. BUT THE TOWER HAS ONE

QUESTION FOR YOU: WILL YOU LEAVE OR WILL YOU STAY?

Think. There was a question.

Bonehead. Choose your ... answer ... wisely.

Don't leave. Don't leave. Stay.

Stay.

"Stay!"

THEN SO BE IT, MY FOOLISH LITTLE ASKER. YOU WERE WARNED.

YOUR TIME.

STARTS.

NOW.

CHAPTER 18

Nine opened her eyes. She was sprawled on the cold stone slabs in the circular room, still clutching Flabberghast's clothes. The horrible laughing in her head slowly faded away. There was another voice.

"Lady? Lady fine?"

Eric's face came unnervingly close to hers and Nine jumped. "Lady always fine," she said, standing up. "Did you hear the Tower's voice?"

"Aye," growled Spoon. "And I did nae like what it was saying."

"Tower mean."

I WOULDN'T WASTE TIME IF I WERE YOU.

Startled, Nine, Eric and Spoon all looked at each other. Spoon drew his sword.

"You heard that?" whispered Nine. The others nodded.

From somewhere up the spiral staircase came a distant wail – a distant, wizardy wail that Nine knew well.

"Flabby!" gasped Eric, his eyes wide with panic, his rough, bark-like hands immediately searching for something in his apron pocket—

He looked round at Nine, crestfallen. "Sweets gone!"

Then there came a distant turnipy kind of wail.

"Gazillion," said Nine and scowled. "Of all the things we need right now, an extra wizard planning revenge is not one of them!" She huffed and, with an armful of cloak, hat and slipper, bounded for the stairs. "Come on."

"Aye," grumbled Spoon, as he and Eric followed her, "makes perfect sense to run towards a pair of wailing wizards up a narrow staircase in a strange tower in a land of magic!"

"We've jumped through a hopscotch grid and been threatened by a building. Nothing has made perfect sense for quite some time!"

Nine leapt up the narrow stairs as fast as she

could. She glanced over her shoulder to see the troll puffing and panting behind her, with Spoon close behind him. Legs feeling the pull of the never-ending stairs, Nine pushed on round the corner, up, up, up.

A sharp, thin voice floated down the stairs. They paused for a moment. It didn't sound like it belonged to a ridiculous wizard or an unturnipped one. It didn't sound wizardy at all…

"Come on!" Nine grabbed Eric's hand, pulling him onwards. Spoon sprinted ahead. A doorway appeared on the left and Nine saw Spoon dash through, sword raised, moustache twitching and kilt flapping.

"We're here, lad! Oh. Why the devil are you—?" Spoon began. Then he was silent.

"Spoon!" yelled Nine, dragging Eric behind her. She was nearly at the room. Fear prickled her mind. Something wasn't right. She turned round to Eric and put a finger to her lips. Then she crept quietly up the last couple of stone steps before the door, took a deep breath – *please don't let this be awful, please don't let this be awful* – and approached the doorway.

The first thing Nine saw in the pentagonal stone-floored room was a dark wooden table on the far side. It was piled high with papers and scrolls. Nine's eyes widened as she saw that behind it sat a strange creature.

It was just a little shorter than herself, Nine guessed, and looked like an eagle: it had feathers, sharp eyes and a beak, but it had feathery arms and hands instead of wings and wore a red-brown tunic on which was pinned a golden feather-shaped brooch. It was scratching away on a piece of parchment with a large feather quill, muttering to itself.

As Nine tiptoed further in, she saw Flabberghast, Gazillion and Spoon, their backs against the wall, their feet not touching the ground, and their hands pinned to it with thick webs. Each of their mouths was covered with the same white, sticky, thready mass, which looked like giant cobwebs spun a thousand times over. Flabberghast and Spoon shot Nine a warning glance. Wide-eyed, Flabberghast shook his head at her.

Eric suddenly moved forwards and peered around the door.

"Found Flabby!" he cried. "Flabby fine?"

"SHHHHH! No more questions!" hissed the eagle-like scribe, slamming down his quill.

Half a dozen large, thick-legged spiders dropped down on threads from the ceiling and grabbed Eric in their strong legs. Before Nine could reach him, the spiders had swung Eric across the room and thrust him against the wall next to Spoon, frantically weaving thick webs over his hands and mouth. Then they shot back up their threads onto a wooden beam that ran across the ceiling.

The eagle creature ignored Nine and continued scratching on its scroll and muttering about Askers. Nine's heart thumped. She stared at the others, now completely helpless. It was up to her. Why was it always up to her?

No more questions…

And yet she had a million questions she needed to ask.

"Hello," she said softly to the creature. It dipped its quill into a bottle of ink, tapped the pen irritably and continued. "You must be fed up with questions," Nine said carefully, her muscles

157

tense, ready for any reaction from the creature or the spiders. She edged further into the room.

"You have no idea," muttered the creature. "Day in, day out people come, all wanting the Tower to answer their pointless questions." It raised its head and scowled at Nine. "They never think of the paperwork it causes for a poor scribe. I've had 302 new entries today! Once people hear the Tower is open for the Hopscotch Championship, everybody wants a turn! It's out of control! We should never have agreed to open again. No wonder the Tower has had enough. I doubt *you* would like to be asked questions all day."

Nine bit her lip. She needed answers … but didn't dare ask him questions.

"It must be awful," she said carefully. "We'll leave you in peace. We'll go…" she examined the creature for any sign of a clue, "further up the Tower."

The creature scratched away furiously with the quill. "You cannot go up the Tower unless you have a key to the door. And you cannot have the key to the door because the Tower must not be disturbed. Hopscotch or no hopscotch!"

"I didn't see a door," she murmured, careful to keep her tone flat and not make it sound like a question. She walked back to the spiralling staircase and looked up the stairs. Definitely no door. She tried to walk up the next step, but her foot knocked into something invisible and solid. Starting from the bottom up, an ancient-looking oak door with black metal studs appeared. Out from the middle of it popped the head of a wooden gargoyle.

"Key," it said in a gruff female voice, and opened its mouth expectantly.

Nine saw the shape of a keyhole inside the gargoyle's mouth.

"I haven't got a key!" she hissed.

The gargoyle's wooden face scrunched up crossly. "Then don't knock on the blimmin' door!" She retreated into the wood, and the door disappeared from the top back down to the bottom, leaving nothing but the stone staircase.

Nine huffed and marched back into the room, feeling her patience vanishing as quickly as the door. She took a deep breath. She needed to stay calm.

"I can see you're really busy," said Nine, walking up to the creature's desk and using every ounce of effort to keep her prickling temper under control. "So if you would be kind enough to release my friends, but *not* that one in the mauve cloak" – she nodded at Gazillion, who wriggled furiously, his blond-green hair flapping about – "then we'll get out of your way."

"There are other reasons to silence you, even if you ask no questions," said the creature, in a warning tone.

"Well, if you were just a little bit helpful, I wouldn't have to keep … not asking!" Nine said, clenching her fists.

The creature slammed its quill down on the table and stood up. It leaned forwards, its feathery hands on the table. Nine's heart skipped a beat. A black iron key hung on a ring fastened to the creature's belt. She could feel that familiar itch in her fingers…

"I am up to my eyes with forms. I haven't had a holiday for ten months. The spiders usually only attack anyone who dares to ask anything, but I'm certain I could persuade them to make an

160

exception." Half a dozen spiders from the ceiling dangled down hopefully. The creature sat down and returned to its paperwork. The spiders looked disappointed and slunk back to their corners.

That's it. No more playing nice.

With the eyes of a professional pickpocket, Nine looked around the room. Key: hanging from belt. Spoon's sword: lying beneath him on floor. Six spiders: ridiculously quick. Victim's weak spot...?

Nine smiled. Oh, yes. She really had missed this...

CHAPTER 19

Nine clenched her fists and then stretched her fingers. Her pre-pounce ritual. *She was the cat, stalking her prey, and she was on in...*

THREE.

She ignored the panicking, muffled squeaks from Flabberghast...

TWO.

She flexed her fingers...

ONE.

She lunged for the desk and, with a sweep of her hand, scattered the papers and scrolls to the floor.

The scribe yelled in protest and stood up, frantically trying to catch the flying parchment. Nine jumped onto the table and, with quick fingers, undid the buckle of the belt and slid off the iron ring with the key.

"How *dare* you?" roared the creature, then clasped its feathery hand over its beak… But it was too late. The question had been asked.

A spider dropped down from the ceiling and began weaving a web to silence him. Nine ducked as three more of the thread-dangling spiders grasped the creature in their strong legs and swung it over to the stone wall, as another spun webs around its hands.

Throwing the key into her satchel, Nine ran over to Spoon and grabbed his sword from the ground. Carefully, she cut away at the strong web pinning Spoon's arm to the wall until his hand was released. He snatched the sword from her hand and in a few quick swipes was free.

The spiders, their work done, climbed lazily back up to the ceiling, just as the freed Spoon dropped to the ground. He pulled at the webs covering his mouth, spitting and spluttering.

"Just don't ask anything!" Nine said, lifting him so he could cut Flabberghast free. The wizard's eyes widened in fear as Spoon sliced away at the webs faster than the spiders had formed them. Moments later, Flabberghast fell gracelessly to the ground – but sprung up quickly, almost joyfully.

"Oho! Well done, Madam!" said Flabberghast, rubbing his wrists. "I always said you were clever."

"You have *never* said I'm clever."

"Yes, well…" He cleared his throat and dropped his voice to a mutter. "Doesn't mean I wasn't thinking it." He quickly put on his hat, cloak and slippers as Nine took Spoon over to free Eric.

"Lady save!" Eric cried, his arms outstretched. He stopped short, as if remembering Nine was not overly fond of hugs, and patted her head awkwardly.

Nine ducked, trying not to catch the troll's expression.

"Free the scribe creature, Spoon," Nine said. She looked at Gazillion. "And cut down this Turnip Brain. I suppose someone with actual magical powers might be useful in this place."

Spoon sliced away at the threads, muttering about one wizard being enough trouble without having two of the blasted things in tow. Nine and Flabberghast slipped out through the doorway and towards the spiral staircase.

"Madam, what in the name of strawberry tea are you doing here?" Flabberghast hissed, as Eric followed and barrelled into him with a huge hug. Flabberghast patted the troll awkwardly on his back.

"You don't think I'm passing up the opportunity to ask a question of my own, do you?" said Nine. "I want to know what my music box is whispering. And besides, we knew you wouldn't get far without us."

"But *how* did you…"

"Well, I stole this little blue skull—"

"You stole a *skull*?!"

"Ignored the other numbers—"

"Ignored the other numbers?!"

"Just jumped straight onto number ten, and here I am."

Flabberghast blinked. "Why didn't we think of that?"

Nine rolled her eyes and reached into her satchel for her music box. She looked over her shoulder to see Gazillion had appeared behind them, pulling webs from his mouth.

"And if *you* so much as try anything..." she began.

"Oh, I wouldn't dream of it," said Gazillion, in a voice that implied he would pretty much try everything.

There was the sound of more web-slicing from the room and then Spoon darted out.

"Impudent Askers," called the creature after them, "I warn you – the Tower will not take kindly to this! On your own heads be it!"

Nine kicked the stone step and the wooden door appeared from the bottom up.

"Key," said the gargoyle, opening her mouth wide.

Nine put the key into the gargoyle's mouth and turned it sharply to the right. There was a *clonk* and a *clank*, and the door disappeared from the top down, the iron key falling from the keyhole and clattering loudly on the stone step before vanishing from sight.

Nine stepped forwards, but a voice spoke in her head.

THE TIMEMASTER HAS THREE GAMES. THE SANDS WILL FALL. AND THEN YOUR TIME WILL END.

"Did you hear that?" Nine whispered to Flabberghast behind her.

"Ohhhh, yes," Flabberghast whispered back. "It appears, Madam, that the Tower has become significantly more bad-tempered since my last visit." He swallowed hard. "And it wasn't the cheeriest soul in the realms to begin with."

"What games will it play?"

"Regretfully, there is no way of knowing, Madam. The Tower is a changeable and dangerous taskmaster. It is all-seeing, all-knowing…"

"And all-grumpy," added Nine.

"I have only succeeded in reaching the Tower twice before. The first time I did not get beyond the entrance hall and the second time… I may have…" Flabberghast glanced at Gazillion.

Nine widened her eyes as the penny dropped. "Did you cheat?"

"Madam!" hissed Flabberghast indignantly. "Cheating is such a … strong word."

"You did cheat."

Flabberghast's cheeks flushed red. "Nowhere did it *specifically* say on the Scroll of Unbreakable Rules that your sister was not allowed to be invisible and ... possibly help you out at certain times. *Nowhere*."

"She helped you?" said Nine incredulously.

"For a hefty price," grumbled Flabberghast.

Nine smiled. "Can she really make herself invisible? She *is* clever."

"She *is* an intolerable show-off," said Flabberghast tightly, and Nine guessed the conversation was closed.

They climbed on in uneasy silence. A definite feeling of chilly unwelcomeness hung in the air, as if even the stone steps were disapproving of yet more Askers and wanted to make life as difficult and unpleasant as possible.

The only sound was the noise of their feet on the stone as they climbed. Other than that, the Tower was silent. Too silent.

If the Tower was bombarded with so many Askers – 302 today – that the poor creature was overwhelmed with paperwork, where were they all?

"Why does the Tower feel so empty?" Nine whispered to Flabberghast.

"I do not know, Madam," Flabberghast whispered back. "It was certainly not so quiet when I was last here."

A little shiver ran down her spine – what *had* happened to the Askers?

"So, you have lost your magic, Flabberghast the Unworthy," Gazillion said, behind Flabberghast, disturbing their thoughts. His voice bubbled with delight. "Rather unfortunate in a place like this, don't you think? That's why the mortal had to bring me along."

"Well, the *mortal* is beginning to wish she'd left that web over your mouth, Turnip Brain," Nine called back to him.

"Ha! It would matter not. A wizard who cannot speak would still be far superior to a wizard who cannot—" Gazillion gasped suddenly, and Nine, Eric and Flabberghast twisted round to see what was wrong. Spoon stood on Gazillion's mauve-cloaked shoulder, his sword against the wizard's throat.

"Choose your words wisely, lad," Spoon

growled, "or you'll soon be a wizard who can neither speak *nor* perform magic."

Another doorway appeared a few steps away, leading into another room.

"Let me check," said Nine, and she kicked the next step past the door—

From the bottom up, another ancient-looking oak door with black metal studs appeared. Out popped the head of the same wooden gargoyle.

"Oh, you again. Key." She opened her mouth.

"What key?"

"The key you retrieved from the mirror, child! Well, the mirror-that-ain't-a-mirror."

"I haven't got a key," said Nine.

The gargoyle huffed. "Then why'd you wake me up? I'm fed up with—"

Nine tutted and moved her foot away from the step. The door disappeared from the top down.

"We need to go in the room," said Nine. "To find that mirror that isn't a mirror. Then I can enjoy shoving the key in that gargoyle's mouth."

Nine took a deep breath and turned to the doorway. "It's time ... to play."

CHAPTER 20

The room was strangely diamond-shaped, and each wall had two mirrors on it – all of different shapes and sizes. In the middle of the room stood a swirly, five-armed iron candle stand, holding five rainbow-flamed candles.

Nine stepped into the room, and immediately sensed movement above her head. She tensed and looked up. A stony forearm stuck out of the wall, and in its fist, an hourglass filled with purple sand. With a grinding sound, the arm turned and tipped the hourglass upside down. Grains of sand began to trickle to the bottom. "The Timemaster is really taking the job seriously," muttered Nine.

"Oh, out of my way, mortal!" barked Gazillion. He pushed past Nine, shoving her into the wall.

Instinctively, Nine stuck out her foot – and smirked as the wizard stumbled into the room. Gazillion glared at her over his shoulder as he moved into the centre.

Nine ignored him and moved towards the five-armed candle stand, fascinated by their rainbow flames. And as she did so, her music box began to whisper again. Strange... Nine strained her ears to hear but it was drowned out by another voice:

THE SANDS ARE FALLING. THE SANDS ARE FALLING. THE SANDS ARE—

"Come now, mirrors!" said Gazillion. "I demand you reveal the hidden key to me, Gazillion the Unstoppable!" He thrust his fingers forwards, wiggling them at the mirrored walls.

Flabberghast, Eric and Spoon peered around the doorframe. Everyone held their breath.

No sparkling mauve threads shot out.

"Oho!" said Flabberghast, sweeping into the room confidently. He walked towards Gazillion and stood beside him, elbowing him as he did so.

Gazillion frowned and thrust his fingers forwards again. "This makes no sense! My power! My beautiful, wonderful power!"

"Ah, my dearest Gazillion the *Unfloppable*, it appears the Tower has muted your magic."

"It's never done that before! This is an outrage!"

"Ah, but where's the challenge? I suppose any fool could blast their way through with magic, could they not?"

"Any fool but you," muttered Spoon.

"I didn't know *this* would happen. This wasn't part of the arrangement," muttered Gazillion, jabbing his fingers out again.

PUFF! The faintest, most pathetic wisp of mauve drifted from one of his fingers and faded into nothing.

"What arrangement?" said Nine. "With who?"

Gazillion looked at Nine and there was a flicker of fear in his eyes. For just a moment, his haughty expression faltered – but then he looked away. "Nothing that concerns you, mortal."

Nine sighed. "Fine. Time is running out and no one has any magic."

"Clearly, Madam, we have to trust our brains," said Flabberghast.

"Your brain?" scoffed Spoon, pointing at Eric. "I'd rather eat Eric's pancakes than trust your brain!"

Eric's face fell again.

"Oh, concentrate!" said Nine to everyone. "The door gargoyle was expecting the key from the mirror-that-isn't-a-mirror. So, we need to work out which one isn't really a mirror."

Nine, the wizards, Eric and Spoon each moved towards a mirror. Spoon jumped up and down on the ground to try to see in his.

"I just see my reflection," said Flabberghast. "This one must be a normal mirror."

Nine stared at her own reflection and stuck out her tongue.

"And this one must be a normal one, too," said Nine, cautiously reaching out her hand towards the glass.

The moment she touched it, she yelped and leapt backwards, because underneath her fingertips, the glass shattered into a million tiny shards, which crumbled to the floor. Everyone gasped and froze.

Then came the silent laugh of the Tower, echoing in their minds. The room became darker.

Nine looked up at the iron candle stand – one of the rainbow-flamed candles had gone out.

They were down to four. She looked back at the smashed mirror; behind the glass was just an empty wooden frame. Then, as if time were working in reverse, all the crumbs of glass picked themselves up and zoomed back into position inside the frame. And there was Nine's reflection once again.

"Eric find. Eric fix," muttered Eric. A look of determination came over his face as he stared at his reflection in a tall, thin mirror on the other side of the room.

"Eric, wait!" began Nine, but Eric poked it with his long yellow fingernail. The glass shattered and crumbled to the floor. Just wood behind the mirror. Another silent laugh. Another candle out. Three to go. Back into the frame the tiny glass crumbs hurtled.

"Eric help!" the troll protested, lumbering to the next mirror.

"Will someone get that foolish creature under control?" roared Gazillion.

Nine, dashed after him, but—

SMASH! Another mirror gone. Another candle out. Two candles left. The room was getting gloomy and Nine could barely see anything. But she could just make out Eric reaching for another mirror...

"Stop, you boulder-brained oaf!" yelled Spoon.

"Not help?" said Eric, his fingernail just an inch away from the glass. "Not fix?" He looked at Nine uncertainly. "Boulder brain?"

Nine took his arm. "We'll find it. Just wait in the middle."

Eric nodded. He turned awkwardly, raising his hand to pat Nine's head. But he didn't get that far. He tripped over his own feet, lunged forwards, his long-nailed hand still extended, and—

SMASH! One candle left. Nine's heart skipped a beat.

"Oops."

"I'll give you 'oops'," growled Spoon.

"Eric silly!" wailed the troll. "Eric spoil!"

"Just ... stay here. And take some deep breaths or something," said Nine, dragging Eric to the middle of the room.

As the downcast troll puffed away noisily, Nine went over to the mirror that Flabberghast stood in front of. It had a blue frame decorated with golden question marks.

"Four mirrors. One chance," said Nine.

"And time is not our friend, Madam!" Flabberghast pointed to the hourglass. The purple sand glowed strangely bright in the gloom. The top was nearly empty.

"There must be something different about the not-a-mirror!" said Nine.

"Aye," said Spoon, hopping over. "It's the only one that holds the key we need!"

Nine stared at the mirror closely, examining the detail of the frame. Looking for any clue in the glass...

"How can you tell if something is glass?"

"Eric smash?"

"Apart from that."

"Reflection," said Spoon.

"They all have that!"

"Touch it," said Gazillion, in front of a black oval mirror. "Cool and hard."

"And we can't do that!" Nine fought the increasing urge to run around the room, smashing the mirrors and yelling in frustration.

Calm. Focus. Breathe.

Just as she'd told Eric...

Breathe.

"BREATHE!"

She leaned closer to the blue-framed mirror she and Flabberghast stood before and breathed out. It steamed up. She ran to the oval mirror in front of Gazillion and breathed out. More steam.

Her heart thumped. Was this it? Had she worked it out? She ran to a gold, swirly-framed rectangular mirror. She breathed out...

And it didn't steam up.

"This one!"

"If you are wrong, mortal, so help me, I'll—"

"It must be!" said Nine.

Please let this be right. Please let this be right.

She held her breath ... reached her fingertip to the mirror ... touched it...

There was the slightest rippling, like dipping a finger in a puddle. Nine's heart leapt to her mouth.

"Time going!" wibbled Eric.

Nine glanced at the hourglass, and the joy of her success disappeared faster than a cup of strawberry tea. The last few grains of sand trickled impatiently down the middle. Nine gritted her teeth and plunged her right hand into the puddle-mirror. Her hand felt weird – as if it belonged to someone else. She grasped around furiously.

It must be here! It must—

Then her fingers closed around something that she could hardly feel. She yanked her hand back out of nothingness and into the room. Her fingers held a key.

"Oho!" crowed Flabberghast. "Well done, Madam! Make haste now!" He grabbed Nine's left arm and dragged her towards the door, with Eric lumbering, Spoon skittering and Gazillion marching right behind.

"Time going!"

A second after they all stepped out of the room, a flaming portcullis dropped from the top of the doorway and slammed into the stone step of the doorway behind them. Everyone froze. Flabberghast and Gazillion exchanged a look.

"Time gone," gulped Eric.

"That's … not at all alarming," said Flabberghast.

Nine walked over to the first step of the staircase and gave it a kick. Up came the door with the gargoyle's head.

"—folks disturbing me, day and night!" finished the gargoyle. She narrowed her eyes in confusion for a moment. "You stop me in the middle of me sentence? Blinkin' Askers! Gimme the blimmin' key!"

With great satisfaction, Nine thrust the key into the gargoyle's mouth and smiled at the key-muffled mutterings of the gargoyle, which probably involved several rude words. The door began to vanish from the top down. The gargoyle scowled at Nine and spat out the key onto her feet, as she and the key both disappeared from view.

"Out of my way," said Gazillion, pushing past Nine and charging up the stairs.

The voice echoed once more in Nine's head as she climbed the steps behind him.

THE SANDS ARE FALLING. THE SANDS ARE FALLING.

CHAPTER 21

Nine couldn't shake the feeling that they were being led into a trap, and yet had no choice but to go on. The only way out was up.

THE SANDS ARE FALLING. YOUR TIME WILL RUN OUT.

Then the voice was silent. There was a door on the left, which Gazillion strutted through without hesitation. As he did so, there came the sound of a stony arm above the door, upturning an hourglass.

The first thing Nine noticed as she stepped into the room was that she couldn't step very far: just inside, a black-bricked wall stretched across the span of the room from wall to wall, so high that it nearly reached the ceiling.

She was squished along as she was joined by Eric, Flabberghast and Spoon. The two wizards elbowed each other edgily and exchanged hateful looks as they stood side by side. Flabberghast reached out, prodded the wall with his little finger and stepped back nervously. Nothing happened.

"It's a wall," he announced.

"Good job we rescued you, lad," said Spoon. "We'd be lost without your valuable insights!"

"To clarify, you didn't *rescue* me!" hissed Flabberghast. "You just *found* me, in a difficult situation, contemplating my next move." He glanced at Gazillion. "Obviously."

"Obviously," said Nine.

"Onwards!" said Gazillion, flicking his hair. "I am burdened with my question!"

"And we are burdened with you," muttered Spoon.

"Turnip question?" said Eric.

"Shhh!" said Nine, Flabberghast and Spoon in unison, as Eric clapped his hands over his mouth. His big yellow eyes blinked above his fingers. Then he slowly lowered his hands, his bark-like cheeks blushing.

"The wall's too high to climb," said Spoon, jiggling restlessly on the spot. "Never breathe a word of this, but someone throw me over."

"I'd be delighted to volunteer," said Flabberghast, pointedly.

"No, it's too high even for that," said Nine.

COME ON, FOOLISH ASKERS. THE SANDS ARE FALLING.

"The key must be beyond this wall. We need to get over it or ... through it..." said Nine. "I wonder..."

Only one way to make a door appear in this ridiculous Tower.

She walked over and kicked the wall – to make herself feel better, if nothing else.

But everyone stared as certain bricks vanished from the bottom up, leaving a large question mark shape in the wall. It was close enough to a doorway and wide enough even for Eric to squeeze through.

"Good," said Nine. "This Tower deserves a good kicking." But despite her bold words, Nine shuddered. Everything was still and silent. The purple grains in the hourglass were flowing fast... She reached inside her satchel and clasped her music box. She longed to know … longed to ask … and they must stop the House hiccupping.

Time to play.

She let the music box drop through her fingers and, with unconvinced legs, she stepped through the vertical line of the question mark.

A flash of cream rectangle – a black circle, filled with lines.

Nine gave a yelp of surprise as the image sprang in front of her eyes. Then, a split-second later, it was gone.

"Madam?!" said Flabberghast. He poked his head through the question mark.

"It's fine," said Nine. "I'm fine. Come in."

She could see the black-bricked walls curving round in an arc in either direction. The walls looked too long and high to fit in the tower room, and yet here they were. Occasional person-width gaps broke up the solid walls, and through them, Nine could see further curved walls – like a circle within a circle within a circle… Like a labyrinth…

Gazillion's head popped through the question mark behind her. His lips curled up in a sneer as if he had just eaten one of Eric's pancakes.

"It's a maze," said Flabberghast.

"Another brilliant deduction, lad!" grumbled Spoon, as the two wizards tried to squeeze through the question mark at the same time. Gazillion popped out the other side first.

A flash of cream rectangle – a black circle, filled with lines.

The strange image appeared again before Nine's eyes and she gasped.

"I know what it is! A map. A map of the labyrinth!" she cried, looking around. "Where is it?"

"No map," said Eric and scratched his head.

"Are you quite all right, Madam?"

Nine frowned. "Didn't you…?"

There it was again – the map filled her vision, but only for the blink of an eye.

The blink of an eye…

Nine felt like she'd swallowed a rock as a terrible thought dropped into her mind. She blinked again. There was the map. She closed her eyes for longer. The entire map was laid out on cream parchment. A circular labyrinth of twists and turns and dead ends.

"The map is inside my eyelids," said Nine, opening her eyes. "Don't any of you have a map?"

"You were first inside the maze, mortal," said Gazillion, oozing smugness. "Maybe that is why you alone bear the burden of Mapbearer."

"So, if we want to see the map," said Flabberghast, "you must have your eyes closed?"

"Looks like it, doesn't it," said Nine. She looked at the curving walls of the maze and had the horrible feeling that this was not going to go well.

THE SANDS ARE FALLING. THE SANDS ARE FALLING. THE SANDS ARE FALLING.

YOUR TIME WILL RUN OUT.

Frustration and fear twisted together inside Nine like the silvery strands of the World Between Worlds.

"Lady back!" Eric tried to pull Nine back towards the question mark. "Not safe!"

Nine shook her arm free, but she hesitated.

"You do not have the courage to face the maze with your eyes shut, do you, mortal?" taunted Gazillion. "Whereas I, Gazillion the Unstoppable, would gladly risk my life—"

"Aye, and I'd gladly risk your life, too," muttered Spoon.

"Because I," continued Gazillion loudly, casting a look at Flabberghast, "have a burning question."

"Turnip!" squeaked Eric, then clasped his hands over his mouth again as everyone – even Gazillion – glared at him.

"You're not the only one with questions!" snapped Nine. "I bet the maze won't make it easy, but I'm not afraid." She looked at Flabberghast, hoping he believed her. "If we can't find out how to stop the House hiccupping, we will lose everything."

Flabberghast looked at Nine, Eric and Spoon with a strange, warm expression. "Not quite everything," he said quietly. And for a brief moment as he looked at them, his eyes sparkled faintly with silver. But then he cleared his throat awkwardly and the moment passed before Nine could understand it. "We are with you every step of the way, Madam."

Somewhere in her head, a Tower laughed and chanted again: THE SANDS ARE FALLING. THE SANDS ARE FALLING.

And the last thing Nine saw as she closed her eyes, was a smile creeping across Gazillion's face.

CHAPTER 22

The map was as clear as if it were on a piece of bone-coloured parchment in front of her. She scanned it with unseeing eyes.

"Well? What do you see, mortal?"

Nine felt a hand impatiently shake her arm. It was followed by the sound of a sword slapping knuckles, and a wizardy growl.

Nine focused on all the black lines – there were surely far too many for a room this size. Round lines, broken lines that stopped and started without warning, twisting back on themselves, and in the middle…

"The key is in the centre," said Nine.

THE SANDS ARE FALLING.

Nine tried to ignore the voice.

YOUR TIME WILL—

"Oh, shut up!" she roared to the Tower, which promptly shut up, possibly more out of surprise than anything else. Her first step was bold, her second was less so. She reached her left hand out and touched the rough brick wall of the labyrinth. Her right hand she put in front of her, feeling wildly in mid-air for any trace of trouble.

There was the familiar light touch of tiny feet landing on one of her shoulders, and a large, rough-skinned hand on the other.

"Eric here," said a small voice, sounding like he very much wished he wasn't. Nine pushed away the urge to hold his hand.

Don't reach for him.

Never. Show. Weakness.

Focus.

She concentrated on the feel of bricks beside her, grounding her, step after step. Coming up was...

"An entrance on our left, Madam. Do we take it?"

Nine traced an imaginary finger on the map. "Yes, this way."

They walked through, then continued right. Nine tried to listen to the others' footsteps on the ground rather than her thumping heart. Partly for reassurance, partly to listen for Gazillion's boots. She didn't trust him one little bit. Nine was stumbling through a maze with her eyes shut in a Tower that wasn't playing nicely, in the company of an unpleasant wizard wanting revenge. But Gazillion was also fearful about something, and Nine really needed to know what. Fearful wizards were dangerous wizards…

They kept walking. Calm and quiet. Too calm and too quiet.

"Er, Madam…" said the wobbly voice of an about-to-panic wizard.

Nine froze. She suspected she was about to find out why exactly it was too calm and too quiet.

"Everything is disappearing behind us!"

"What?!" Nine could only resist for a second before opening her eyes and turning around.

In the distance, the walls were simply vanishing, and everything was turning cream, like a blank piece of parchment. It was being erased. The vanishing grew closer and closer.

She shut her eyes again and felt as if she'd been punched in the stomach. The map of the labyrinth inside her eyelids was also vanishing – shrinking from the outside in.

"No!" said Nine, squeezing her eyes tightly shut. "RUN!" Then, as fast as she dared, she ran, trying to work out the route as she went, brushing the walls with her left hand, to ground herself while her brain shrieked at her to stop running blind.

"Left!" She slowed down as she entered the doorway. "Left again!"

It was like running the streets of the town as a pickpocket, her latest prize in her hand, voices yelling, footsteps thumping behind her, except this time it wasn't just *her* life that was at stake.

"You'd better be right, lass," said Spoon, grabbing a handful of her short, spiky hair.

"Hurry, mortal!"

"It's disappearing right behind me, Madam!" said the wobbly voice of a definitely panicking wizard.

Focus. Focus. No time for mistakes.

"Left again! No... Wait, go right ... no..."

Panic rushed through her like a flood, her legs refusing to move. A cold dread hit her chest.

"Faster, mortal! Which way?"

No time—

"Mortal!"

"Oh, everyone shut up!" yelled Nine, beyond bothering to keep the panic from her voice. She put her hands to her head. *Turn left next – that will take us to that line... Then go right... No, that's a dead end... Turn left again... Dead end. Dead end. DEAD END.*

"The walls beside me are going!" wailed Flabberghast.

"Lady help!"

THE SANDS ARE FALLING. THE SANDS ARE FALLING.

FOCUS.

"We can't outrun it, lass," Spoon said in her ear. "You did your best."

Go down that line ... and...

"TURN RIGHT! We can get to the inner circle!"

"MADAM!" Flabberghast let out an ear-splitting screech.

Unable to bear it, Nine opened her eyes

and whirled around. The walls beside the beyond-panicking wizard had gone. The cream nothingness was everywhere. Flabberghast had frozen in terror. His auburn hair, his indigo cloak, his pyjamas, slippers, everything turning cream, as if he, too, was becoming part of the bone-coloured parchment of the map. He started falling – fading – backwards, the outline of his body disappearing, merging with the cream.

"Flabby stay!" wailed Eric, pulling him forwards, a step away from the vanishing walls. Flabberghast collapsed, pale as bone, as Eric scooped him up in his arms. Spoon tugged Nine's hair.

"Run, lass!"

Nine closed her eyes and ran, turning right through the doorway...

That should bring us to...

Nine opened her eyes and saw ... the inner brick-walled circle of the labyrinth.

Everything behind them had vanished. Only the inner circle was left. And there was the key in the centre, lying on the parchment ground. Everyone piled in behind Nine, nudging her forwards. Eric dropped Flabberghast in an undignified heap.

"Thank you," the wizard muttered, as Eric hauled him to his shaky feet.

Spoon leapt down from Nine's shoulder towards the key, his little fingers outstretched, grasping its looped head as...

Gazillion's boot slammed down on top of the key, forcing it to the ground. "I'll take that," he said.

Spoon held his gaze for a moment, then reluctantly moved his fingers away from the key. "I'm watching you," he said, then stabbed Gazillion's ankle.

The unturnipped wizard yelped, snatched the key and stared back at Spoon. "And I, Doctor, am watching you."

There was an uneasy silence.

"Shall we?" said Gazillion, holding the key aloft. "Two challenges down, one to go. Our answers are within reach."

He walked out of the inner circle. As he did so, the wall circle and the parchment ground slowly faded away, leaving just the stone floor of the hexagonal tower room beneath their feet.

Flabberghast walked over to Nine and put a hand on her shoulder. He gave a nod and a small smile, then cautiously followed Gazillion. Eric trundled after him as Spoon hopped up onto Nine's shoulder.

"We should have left him webbed up," murmured Spoon.

Nine stopped still as thoughts connected in her mind. "Have you … ever met him before?"

"Never seen the flamin' wizard before today, and I never want to see him *after* today."

"Then … how does he know you're a doctor?" Nine whispered back. Spoon frowned.

The wizards and Eric left the room. Nine followed slowly behind.

She wished she had never been magicked by the banister in the House. Wished that her music box hadn't whispered. Wished she could ignore this burning, all-consuming hunger to know…

Nine reached the doorway, in time to hear a gruff little voice say, "Still goin', eh? Never mind, I doubt you'll make it through the next one. The Tower always wins, you know. Then, *finally*, I'll get some peace and—"

Gazillion clamped his hand over the gargoyle's mouth. There was silence for a moment, then the gargoyle's muffled voice said, "Key."

Gazillion removed his hand and the gargoyle grumpily opened her mouth. The wizard inserted the key and turned it. There was a clonk, a clank, and the door vanished, the key clattering onto the stone step before fading away. Then, followed by Flabberghast and Eric, Gazillion began to climb the stairs.

"You know Flabberghast said he thought coming here was a mistake?" said Nine to Spoon. "Don't ever tell him this, but I agree with him." Nonetheless, she thought of the House and began to climb the stairs.

CHAPTER 23

Every step felt like a thousand as Nine's heavy legs trudged up the seemingly endless stairs. She focused on Eric's rope-like tail, swinging like a pendulum from left to right as he climbed in front of her.

Nine had an overwhelming desire to reach out to him as they trudged higher and deeper into this strange, unnerving building.

No. Never. Show. Weakness. Never…

But Nine couldn't resist. She reached out and touched his tail, holding it gently in her hand. The troll gasped and turned around. Seeing Nine, his face relaxed and he smiled.

"Eric here," he said. "Lady safe."

"You mean, 'Lady here, Eric safe,'" said Nine,

letting his tail softly fall between her fingers.

"Gazillion here," muttered Spoon in her ear, "no one safe."

"I wonder if the House is safe," said Nine, biting her lip. She pushed away the image of an hourglass above the House, the purple sand trickling down…

Above them, there was another doorway leading from the staircase. Nine didn't bother to kick the stone step beyond it. She knew what was waiting there. So she stepped through and the stony arm above her turned the hourglass upside down.

Flabberghast, Gazillion and Eric were already standing in an eight-sided room. This one was different from all the others. It had nothing in it at all.

Or did it? There *was* something. Something Nine couldn't see. Something she could feel. She looked over her shoulder, as if she was expecting the stone walls to be creeping up on her. But there was nothing.

"Not like," said Eric, wringing his tail.

Nine balled her fists. She didn't know who –

or what – she was meant to be fighting, but she had not come this far to fail.

"Something's wrong," she said quietly.

"Aye, there's devilry here," muttered Spoon, jumping down from Nine's shoulder. He slowly rotated on the spot, his sword pointing to every stone in the wall as he turned.

I AM THE TIMEMASTER.

No one said anything. There was just silence. Endless, awful, terrifying silence. Until the Tower broke it with a whisper.

AND YOU'LL RUN OUT OF TIME. THEY ALWAYS RUN OUT OF TIME.

They… The other Askers…

The thought that had been prickling away at Nine's mind flared up again. She turned to Flabberghast. "We're so far into the Tower and we still haven't seen a soul. All those hundreds of people that the scribe said had come," she whispered. "They must be somewhere!"

"It's like the floor just swallowed them up." Flabberghast looked around him nervously.

Nine stared at the wall again. A little shiver ran down her spine. There was something …

something they couldn't see … something they were missing… She crept towards the wall, her heart thumping, a chill spreading from her chest. She reached out a finger and poked one of the large stones.

Suddenly, an eye opened in the middle of the stone and stared at her. Nine screamed and jumped backwards. Then eye after eye after eye popped open in every stone in the wall, from floor to ceiling, until they were surrounded by hundreds – maybe thousands – of seeing stones.

"Swallowed up… The people who went before… What if they're not just *in* the Tower!" cried Nine, as a feeling of horror shot through her. "What if they *are* the Tower?!" She looked at the seeing stones. "Close your eyes now if you're the Askers," she called to the wall.

Nine felt like her stomach had disappeared as the hundreds of eyes vanished in the stones.

No… Oh no…

Then all the eyes opened again and stared at Nine from the stones.

THEY *ALWAYS* RUN OUT OF TIME! And the Tower's voice roared with laughter.

"Eric scared."

"That's where everybody went? This Tower has truly taken leave of its senses! We must go!" said Flabberghast.

He grabbed Nine with one hand and Eric with the other, and ran to the doorway.

They slammed into something invisible. A wooden door appeared from the bottom up with the gargoyle's face frowning at them.

"Oh, for cryin' out loud," she grumbled. "Didn't you realise you actually need the *key* before I can let you leave the room? Blimey, they let *anyone* in these days."

Nine wedged her foot firmly against the door, trying to ignore the hundreds of eyes staring at her back.

"And 'cause you tried to leave without it, I have to be the door to this room now. Them's the rules. Thanks for nothin'. I hate this room – it's horrible. All these Askers. Stuck here for ever, like me."

A thought struck Nine and she pushed her foot harder against the door to make sure it didn't disappear. "You weren't always a keyhole?"

"Wanted to ask the Tower if I should travel the worlds or stay perched on me castle wall." The gargoyle sighed as Nine anxiously looked over her shoulder. Hundreds of eyes stared back. "Now I'm stuck in a Tower answerin' the door to fools."

"You could have warned us!" cried Nine.

"Not my problem. Now, move your blimmin' foot. I hate watchin' this next bit."

"Next bit?" said Flabberghast sharply.

"You've spent so long natterin' to me, it's gonna happen any second now."

"What?" cried Flabberghast. "What will happen?"

The gargoyle raised her eyes towards the hourglass above her. "Well, you're halfway through now. The arms are about to wake up, ain't they?"

"Arms?" said Nine, casting a panicked look at the staring stones.

Suddenly, a pair of grey, stony arms shot out of the Tower wall near the doorway, where Eric stood close to the wall. They wrapped themselves around the troll, grasping him tightly. Nine gasped. She and Flabberghast went to grab him.

No – NO!

Before anyone could do anything, the arms pulled the troll into the wall, leaving nothing but a pair of wide, sad, yellow eyes in the stone.

CHAPTER 24

"ERIC!" screamed Nine, taking her foot away.

"'Ere we go," muttered the gargoyle as she vanished.

Nine and Flabberghast ran over to Eric's stone. Nine's legs gave way, and she crumpled to the wooden floorboards. Eric's eyes blinked. Nine reached up and put her hands on his stone, unsure if she was going to vomit or scream. Her heart felt like it had been ripped out of her chest. Her head buzzed and the world wasn't there any more.

She was vaguely aware of gentle hands on her shoulders. "Madam…" said a shaky voice. "MADAM!"

Arms reached around her from behind, pulled her away from the wall and into the middle of the room. A bolt of panic shot through Nine, and she kicked, screamed and wrestled – until she realised the arms were covered in indigo material. Nine spun around.

"Get him back!" she roared at Flabberghast, wrestling free of his grip. "Get him back!"

The wizard's eyes filled with tears, and his face was grim. "Madam," he said quietly, in a breaking voice, "I cannot."

"This is all your fault!" Nine shouted. "You and that stupid House! I wish I'd never met you!"

Gazillion's eyes were wide and fearful, and he jumped as Nine whirled around to him.

"And you!" she cried, tears blurring her vision. "Gazillion the Unstoppable, with your unstoppable flouncing and snarling and sneering! You think you're so much better than everyone. You're not. He may be Flabberghast the Unworthy, but he's worth ten of you!"

"How dare you!"

"You don't deserve to be anything other than a turnip! And I hope you never find out who did it!"

But Gazillion just smirked. "Ha! You still think this is about turnips? I pity you, mortal." The fear flickered in his eyes again and he dropped his voice to a whisper. "You know nothing."

Nine's body tensed. She had the overwhelming urge to punch his face. Her right arm shook, she clenched her fist tighter, moved her arm back a little and—

Spoon jumped on Nine's shoulder. She felt a tiny wooden hand rest on her cheek. "Easy, lass. We may need him yet."

Nine held back her punch, then dropped her arm, painful, shallow breaths still bursting out of her. Hatred burned in Gazillion's eyes.

"We need to find that key," said Spoon, "or we'll be naught but eyes ourselves. The arms are back." He pointed up at the hourglass which was running out of sand.

Nine blinked her eyes, wiped her nose on the back of her hand. She looked around the room, avoiding Eric's stone.

It wasn't real. It couldn't be real. Everything inside her burned.

Out of various stones, arms were growing out a little way, and reaching out as if to grab something – someone – and then disappearing back into the wall. Moments later, they reached out again, further into the octagonal room.

"They are getting closer," said Flabberghast. "Every time they come out of the wall. Gah! this is impossible! And we still have no clue where the key is!"

Nine glanced at the doorway, then decisively grabbed Spoon from her shoulder and hurled him at Flabberghast. The wizard caught him with surprised, fumbling fingers. Then Nine marched to the doorway and booted it sharply.

Arms came out of the wall near the door, grasping wildly, but not yet reaching her. Up came the door, with the gargoyle tutting and rolling her eyes.

"Right, if you ain't got the key this time, so help me, I'll—"

"Where is it?"

"I ain't helpin' you! Blimey, my head would roll! And that's all I got left!"

"We need help! Tell me where it is!"

The arms reached closer.

"Madam," said Flabberghast, his voice edged with fear.

"No!" retorted Nine.

"Madam, get back!"

"NO!" she said, staring at the gargoyle. "Help us!"

The arms reached closer.

"I ain't helpin' no Askers," the gargoyle whispered. "The Tower is all-seein', all-knowin'. It wants revenge on the Askers and I ain't bein' on the receivin' end again!"

An arm reached for Nine, and she dodged its outstretched fingertips, watching as it vanished back into the wall. It bounced again almost immediately – grasping furiously in the air, hurtling towards her.

"MADAM!"

Arms were nearly reaching everyone in the middle of the room. Gazillion and Flabberghast kept trying to hide behind each other. One more bounce out from the wall and the arms would grab them both.

"What if it doesn't get revenge? Not this time! I'll free you!" Nine blurted out desperately. "I'll ask the Tower how. With my question!"

The gargoyle narrowed her eyes. "You're lyin'."

"On your left, lass!" bellowed Spoon.

An arm darted towards Nine. Her eyes widened as it nearly reached her, but she couldn't take her foot away.

"You promise on somethin'!"

Nine's fingers reached for her music box inside her satchel, just as fingers from the arm reached for her waist. She lifted the music box to the gargoyle's face.

"This means the world to me! And I promise on this we will free you!" Desperate – defeated – with nothing else she could give.

Purple grains trickling down the hourglass – fingertips reaching her. Nine had no choice but to move her foot.

The door began disappearing from the bottom up. Nine dashed to the middle of the room, where Flabberghast grasped her elbow and Spoon jumped onto her shoulder.

The gargoyle's face creased up anxiously. "Look for the closed fist!" she whispered, as her chin vanished. "Won't make no difference, though..."

The door had nearly disappeared.

"...'cause in the next room—"

The gargoyle had gone.

"Aha!" Gazillion said, pointing at an arm moving towards them. Instead of searching fingers, it had a balled fist. "You get it, mortal!" He shoved Nine towards it.

"Nay! This one's mine!" cried Spoon, swishing his sword. "For Professor Dish! Yaaaaahhhhh!"

Before Nine could move, he charged for the fist.

CHAPTER 25

Nine, Flabberghast and Gazillion all squished closer together in the centre. A couple of arms that were reaching out from the far wall towards them suddenly stopped as Spoon darted beneath them. Their fingers pointed down towards him, as if trying to work out what had happened.

Nine gasped as she felt fingertips brush her satchel. She looked left to see a long, stony arm reaching desperately, but not quite able to grasp her. It bounced back towards the wall.

Don't look.

Just ... don't look...

"MAKE HASTE, MADAM!"

Nine held her breath as she watched Spoon roll into a ball beneath the reaching arms, causing the hands to snatch at air. He ran underneath the balled fist and reached up, stabbing furiously with his tiny sword.

"Come on, Spoon!" Nine called. She couldn't bear the thought of him being caught, too. She risked a little glance towards the pair of sad yellow eyes. They stared back at Nine. She looked away, unable to handle the rush of guilt – loneliness – grief – everything that flooded her.

She focused on Spoon, still rolling and darting and dodging the stony hands slamming down left and right around him.

"The arms are back! This is our last chance!" warned Flabberghast.

Spoon leapt up on top of the balled fist, jumping up and down wildly. The fist shook from side to side. Spoon clung to the wrist, legs dangling. His tiny sword clattered to the floor, but he swung his legs up, kicking the fist mercilessly from underneath.

The fist had had enough. It threw itself open – a key clattered to the floor. Spoon hurtled down, grabbing his sword in one hand and the key in the other.

"I have it!" he said.

"To me!" Nine stretched out her hand as Spoon launched himself towards her, throwing the key. Nine was about to catch it, when Gazillion leaned forwards and scooped the key out of the air. He smirked.

"Give it here!" shouted Nine, but just at that moment, a stony arm reached for Gazillion. He shrieked and the key dropped from his hand. Nine dived for it and scrambled to the doorway. She kicked out desperately. The arms bounced towards her.

The door reappeared from the bottom.

"Quicker!" Nine yelled at the door.

The gargoyle appeared. "You promise?" she demanded. "You promise you'll free me?"

"MADAM!" shrieked Flabberghast. Stony arms grabbed his waist.

"YES!" Nine cried, her heart breaking as the hope of learning the secret of her music box floated away. She looked back, as Flabberghast was dragged towards the wall. "I PROMISE! QUICK!"

"Key."

With trembling, fumbling hands, Nine stuffed the key into the gargoyle's mouth, as Flabberghast yelled, "HELP M—!"

Silence.

Flabberghast!

Had they made it? Nine turned around, heart thumping. Flabberghast sat on the floor, his back against the wall, the stony arms still around his waist. Then the arms released him and calmly retreated into the stone wall.

Flabberghast sat there panting and wide-eyed.

"I'll be watchin' you," said the gargoyle, and vanished with the door.

There was a little clunk as the key dropped to the floorboards, then disappeared. Nine stared as Spoon bounded over to Flabberghast.

"On your feet, lad," he said. "Unwise to linger."

"Dr Spoon," panted Flabberghast. "You're … not a failure."

"Aye, and you're no fool." He twisted his moustache thoughtfully. "Apart from dealing with green-horned minotaurs. Then, lad, you're the greatest fool I know."

Flabberghast gave the briefest flicker of an exhausted smile.

Gazillion walked over to the doorway. The half-smile passed across his face again but Nine had no words or energy left to stop him as he dashed past her and up the stone steps.

The Tower laughed again. I AM THE TIMEMASTER. THEY ALWAYS RUN OUT OF TIME.

Nine forced herself to look at Eric's eyes, which blinked at her sadly. Slowly, she made her way towards them on legs that felt heavy as rocks.

"I'm so sorry," she whispered, her voice breaking. "Why is it always you?"

"He has the smallest brain," said Spoon, in a voice that was strangely soft.

"And the biggest heart," said Flabberghast from somewhere behind her.

Nine reached her fingers towards Eric but couldn't bear to touch the stone. Her fingers stayed outstretched for a moment, then her hand dropped hopelessly to her side.

Flabberghast appeared beside her. He rested

his fingertips on the stone, then sniffed loudly and wiped his nose with his sleeve. He unpinned his cloak, wrapped it around Nine and fastened it. "Madam, we must go," he said in a choked voice.

Nine pulled the cloak tightly around herself, wishing it could somehow protect her from all this. She didn't resist as Flabberghast put his hands on her shoulders and steered her gently but urgently to the door. The world had dissolved around her into something that didn't make sense any more. She'd lost Eric; she'd lost her chance to find out the truth about her music box. Everything felt numb and pointless. The only feeling, as she walked up the stone steps, was Flabberghast's hand in the small of her back, pushing her ever onwards.

Spoon hopped up onto her shoulder. "Head up, lass," he said, breaking into her dazed, foggy thoughts. "And mind sharp. We don't know what waits around the corner."

"Whatever it is," said Flabberghast behind Nine, "I doubt we want Gazillion to be alone with it for long. We ask our questions. We get out. Once he knows who turnipped him, I do not think it wise to linger."

The chanting began as a whisper:

THE SANDS ARE FALLING. THE SANDS ARE FALLING…

Getting louder…

THE SANDS ARE FALLING. THE SANDS ARE FALLING…

And louder…

THE SANDS ARE FALLING. THE SANDS ARE FALLING!

The stone staircase stopped abruptly at the doorway of a room on the left. A tall wooden ladder propped against the last stone step reached up through a hole in the roof.

I AM THE TIMEMASTER!

And then … there was silence.

"Timemaster or not," said Spoon, running up the last steps towards the doorway, "no one takes a troll without my permission. Let's give this Tower a good kick up the—"

The movement broke Nine out of her clouded thoughts. "No – Spoon!"

"It's deathly quiet!" hissed Flabberghast,

grabbing Spoon just before he entered the room. Spoon wriggled furiously. "What have we learned about rooms that are deathly quiet?! We're not losing you, too."

Spoon stopped wriggling and Flabberghast put him down.

"Now," said Flabberghast, "we're at the top of the Tower. I don't know what final trick it has up its sleeve."

I DO, whispered back the Tower smugly.

Flabberghast gritted his teeth. "Just everybody … be careful." He swallowed and held his head high. "For our House. For our home."

"For Professor Dish."

Nine hugged her satchel under the cloak and thought of her music box. She pushed away the screaming sadness. "For a promise."

Then she pulled the cloak more tightly around her and peered through the doorway.

CHAPTER 26

Nine could see an upright, amber oval stone about half her size. It pulsated angrily from every angle of its chiselled surface. It was odd to say an amber stone didn't feel friendly, but there was no doubt in Nine's mind that it didn't want them there. Resentment poured from it – but Nine poured more back in. This Tower, and the Stone behind it, had taken everything – everything – from her.

"That is the Asking Stone," whispered Flabberghast.

Spoon hopped up onto Nine's arm, and slid down it, landing in her palm. Flabberghast's fluffy slippers shuffled slightly on the stone steps behind her.

"After you, Madam?" he squeaked.

"I'm always going first. It's your turn," said Nine.

"Together," said Spoon.

Nine and Flabberghast looked at him for a moment, then looked at each other, and exchanged a nod. Flabberghast moved alongside Nine, then, squished together side by side, they stepped through the thick-walled, stone doorway.

As they did so, Nine's breath was snatched away. It felt like she was trapped in a very strange rectangular bubble. Instinctively, she put her hands up, throwing off Spoon, who landed neatly at her feet.

"It's like … glass?" said Nine. "We're inside glass?"

Spoon reached out and tapped the case with his sword. It made a high, tinging sound.

"Aye."

Flabberghast banged his fists against the glass. "Clearly the Tower is beyond all reason! Let us out!"

I AM THE TIMEMASTER. HERE I CONTROL TIME.

Suddenly the glass case slid forwards into the room, like a playing piece on a board. As it did so, the rectangular shape popped outwards into a large, rounded bubble shape. Nine gasped as a narrow pillar shot up through the floorboards to the left of them – just outside, but not touching, the bubble. And another to the right. And then one more behind them.

AND *YOUR* TIME HAS COME TO AN END.

Nine began to breathe quickly. A sense of panic began rising in her chest. She slammed her hands against the glass—

But the bubble slid around the wall to the right.

"Oh no," murmured Flabberghast.

Nine followed his gaze and her stomach lurched. Curving round the room was a row of large hourglasses, their bottom halves filled with purple sand. And in the hourglass next to them was Gazillion, already waist high in sand, which rained down upon his head. His eyes were wide with panic and he yelled silent words to them as he slammed his hands pointlessly against the glass. Then he pointed at something above their heads.

And purple sand began to pour down on them.

SEE, FOOLISH ASKERS? YOUR TIME HAS RUN OUT!

"Let us out! Let us out!" Flabberghast yelled, slamming his hands against the glass.

NO. REVENGE IS MINE. NO MORE ASKERS. NO MORE QUESTIONS.

Spoon began thwacking the glass with his sword. Nine grabbed her satchel and began bashing it against the bubble. Her thoughts turned painfully to Eric. If only they had his strength now. He was stronger than all of them put together.

Nine paused as the sand rose past her ankles.

"Together," she said.

"What?" said Flabberghast, turning to face her.

"Push it together! Maybe we can topple it."

She batted the cloak to one side and slammed her full body weight against the glass globe, her thoughts on Eric as the impact sent shockwaves through her body. A second after her, Flabberghast threw himself forwards. Spoon, waist high in sand, waded over to the edge and pushed with his spindly arms. The hourglass wobbled.

WAIT… WHAT ARE YOU DOING?

"It needs to be at the same time!" said Nine.

"Don't mention time!" snapped Spoon, as the sand poured down.

"Three … two … one … now!" said Nine.

She slammed her body against the glass once more, as the wizard and the spoon did the same.

STOP! I'M THE TIMEMASTER.

"Now!" Nine threw herself against the glass, silently screaming her desperate questions.

Why did he have to be taken?

"Now!"

Why did I let myself care?

Spoon let out a roar of frustration. Nine looked down and saw he was up to his chin, unable to move. She reached down, grabbed him and threw him on Flabberghast's shoulder.

"Now!"

Why am I trapped in a promise?

The sand had reached her knees.

"Now!"

Her music box jolted inside her satchel.

Why did it have to be this way?

Their hourglass rocked forwards … lingered for just a moment … then rocked back again.

STOP! I AM THE TIMEMASTER! YOU'RE

NOT MEANT TO BE IN THERE TOGETHER!

She glanced sideways at Gazillion. His eyes were wide and desperate.

"Tough!" Nine yelled. "Because we *are* together. And *together* is how we survive! Now!"

It rocked forwards again … lingered…

I – CONTROL – TIME!

…then the hourglass toppled forwards with a stomach-lurching tilt and smashed on the floorboards.

They tumbled out in a heap amongst the shards of glass and sand. Nine felt a sharp scratch on her hand. As they staggered to their feet, she saw it was bleeding. She quickly grabbed a fold of the cloak and pressed down on the cut.

"You might control time," yelled Nine, the pain from the cut fuelling her anger, "but you don't control me!"

"Let's ask the questions and get out of this flamin' death trap," said Spoon, marching over to the Asking Stone.

Nine and Flabberghast both looked back at Gazillion. The sand had nearly covered his mouth. They looked at each other.

"You cannae be serious?" said Spoon, his little mouth hanging open.

But Nine and Flabberghast ran over to the wizard's hourglass. They each grabbed one of the poles that ran either side of the glass bubble, and pulled – and pulled...

ARGH! YOU ARE NOT MEANT TO TOUCH THAT EITHER. YOU ARE CHEATING. YOU ARE ABSOLUTELY CHEATING.

They could no longer see Gazillion's mouth. They pulled and pulled – and pulled...

CRASH! Down toppled the hourglass, smashing the glass and sending Gazillion spilling out in a sea of sand and landing at Spoon's feet, gasping for air. Spoon was ready, his sword outstretched. The wizard came to a halt with the sword a fingernail's width from his nose.

"Any nonsense," said Spoon, "and you're dead."

Gazillion stood up, glaring at Spoon. Then his gaze drifted over towards the Asking Stone.

"We won," Nine announced to the Tower. "We won your games. You have to answer us."

I'M NOT PLAYING ANY MORE.

"You have to," said Nine. "Or we'll tell everyone

you're a useless stone and that we survived the Tower and then everyone will come and there'll be thousands and—"

FINE! FINE! BUT I'M STILL THE TIMEMASTER AND I … NEARLY ALWAYS CONTROL TIME. ONE QUESTION AND ONE QUESTION ONLY. AND MAKE IT QUICK. YOU'VE GIVEN ME A HEADACHE.

Gazillion strutted closer to the throbbing amber Stone.

"Oh no you don't, laddie," said Spoon. "My turn first!"

"I think not!" said Gazillion. "I've waited a long time for this!"

Flabberghast looked at Gazillion, wide-eyed and worried.

Spoon and Gazillion pushed and jostled each other as they stood in front of the Stone.

COME ON. ASK.

The wizard and spoon glared at each other, then both asked at the same time:

"Where is Professor—?"

Spoon stopped in surprise.

Gazillion finished, "—Dish?"

CHAPTER 27

Everyone stared at Gazillion.

"Why—?" began Nine, but Flabberghast clapped his hand over her mouth.

"Do not waste your question, Madam!"

The Stone throbbed.

BEYOND.

Beyond ... what?

Spoon frowned in confusion, but Gazillion smirked. He quickly turned, raised his turnip-coloured trouser leg ... and with a quick flick, he booted Spoon across the room, sending him crashing into an hourglass.

"I haven't forgotten you," Gazillion said, pointing at Flabberghast. "I will find you and I will fry you. But you can wait. For I —" he tossed his greenish hair – "have pressing business to attend to." Then he flounced out of the room.

Spoon stood up, dizzily, and started to run after him. "Spoon!" called Nine. "You didn't finish your question! Maybe the Stone only answered Gazillion!"

Spoon dashed back to the Stone. "And how the devil do we stop that flamin' House from hiccupping so we can find Dish?"

TICKLE.

Spoon nodded at the sulky Stone, then sprinted for the doorway. "Back here, Turnip Head! I've got questions for YOU!"

Nine was torn, wanting to chase after him, but she had come all this way with a question…

Flabberghast stepped closer to the Stone. Its amber glow lit up his face.

"Come on! Ask your question! We must get back to the House!" said Nine. Then she frowned. "But … now we know how to stop the House hiccupping…"

"I can ask something else." Flabberghast stared at the Stone. "I could ask how to restore my magic. Then I could win the hopscotch," he murmured.

"Prove myself. No longer be Flabberghast the Unworthy."

"I don't think you're unworthy," said Nine. "And neither did Eric." She pulled her music box out of her satchel. She thought of the yellow eyes in the wall. It was unbearable. She pulled Flabberghast's cloak more tightly around her shoulders. Her throat tightened. She had a promise to keep.

"I'm sorry about your music box, Madam," said Flabberghast.

Nine nodded. All the feelings she had tried so hard to push back while they fought for their lives now threatened to rise up like a tide inside her. To overwhelm her. Defeat her. Tears were burning, pushing behind her eyes, and Nine knew if they fell, they would fall for ever.

OH, GET ON WITH IT!

"Shut up!" roared Nine, her sadness twisting into anger.

YOU CAN'T SHOUT AT ME. I AM IN CONTROL!

Flabberghast looked at the Stone. "Yes, about that," he said. "I really don't think you are any more."

WHAT?

"How do I free everyone in this Tower?" Flabberghast asked. Nine turned and stared at him. "That is my question."

WHAT?! The Asking Stone groaned.

"That was *my* question!" said Nine.

"Answer me!" Flabberghast bellowed at the Stone.

FOR CRYING OUT LOUD! BLUE.

"Blue," said Flabberghast with a frown. "I have no idea what that—"

NEXT. MAKE IT QUICK. I AM REALLY NOT IN A GOOD MOOD.

Nine's heart thumped.

It was her turn, but … she didn't need to ask about the gargoyle! Her promise was fulfilled. She could ask… She could ask…

She stared boldly into the Stone. "How can I find out what my music box is saying?"

BURN.

THERE. DONE. HAPPY NOW? GO AWAY, HORRID LITTLE CREATURES.

The amber oval stopped pulsating.

"What … but … is that it?" said Nine, heat

inside her rising. "One word? Aren't you going to tell us what to do with these words?"

"There must be more," said Flabberghast. "There used to be more!"

NO. CLEAR OFF.

"No! Wait!" cried Nine. "All this for 'tickle' and 'blue' and 'burn'?" The yellow eyes in the wall were bursting her heart. "You need to explain!"

I REALLY DON'T.

"None of that even makes sense! We lost everything! Talk to me!"

I'M NOT TALKING ANY MORE.

The deafening silence of a definitely-not-talking Asking Stone.

Fury erupting inside, Nine kicked out at the Stone. As soon as she did, she and Flabberghast were blasted across the other side of the room. Nine landed hard on the floorboards, the cloak flapping over her.

"Madam, we should leave before we make matters worse," said Flabberghast, standing up immediately.

"Worse?!" bellowed Nine. "How can they possibly be worse?"

Flabberghast pulled Nine up and steered her towards the door.

"And stop pushing me around!" shouted Nine, fighting off his hands. "Don't touch me!"

She should never have allowed herself to care. Not about the troll. Not about the music box. Not about the House.

Not about anything.

Tears blurred her vision. "That's what we get? We still don't know how to fix the House! We lost everything! Everything!"

Life does bring you strawberries. And then it takes them away...

She threw the music box down onto the floor in front of the Asking Stone and stormed out of the room. A smug voice whispered after her.

TOLD YOU I WAS IN CONTROL. FOOLISH ASKERS.

Nine stood outside the doorway and wiped tears away. Tears that she could no longer force back. She stared at the wooden ladder with unfocused eyes. She just wanted to kick until every inch of her was broken and exhausted and empty...

"Aaaaaaaaargh!" A distant, agonised wail came

from the top of the ladder, breaking through Nine's thoughts.

Spoon!

Flabberghast dashed past her and began to climb. Nine followed, as quickly as she could.

Let him be all right … let him be all right. No, don't care about him … don't care … shut it down … shut it DOWN.

Hot on Flabberghast's heels, Nine crawled through the small doorway at the top of the ladder. She was inside the pointed roof of the Tower – a wide, round room with a stone-lined ceiling spiralling up to a narrow point, supported by wooden beams.

No Spoon.

Seven translucent circles – one of each colour of the rainbow – were dotted around the room. They were as tall and wide as Nine, and whooshing around the hazy edge of each circle was a crackling silvery light, like magical wheels somehow in motion, except the circles didn't move. Gazillion stood by the green circle, peering into it thoughtfully. He had a bleeding nose and little slashes in his cloak.

"Where's Spoon?" Nine demanded, coming to stand beside Flabberghast.

"I think we've had enough questions, mortal, don't you?" sneered Gazillion. "See you back at the Hopscotch Championship, Flabberghast the Unworthy. I'll look forward to that. After all, *my* powers will be restored once I leave the Tower." He flashed them a half-smile, jumped through the green circle, and disappeared.

As he did so, they saw Spoon lying on the ground, behind where Gazillion had stood, the sword close to his outstretched, motionless hand.

CHAPTER 28

"Spoon!" cried Nine, as they dashed forwards. Flabberghast scooped him up. Spoon's tiny limbs draped floppily over the wizard's hands.

Nine prodded him. The spoon gave a little moan, rolled his head to the side, and then was still.

The silvery crackling running around all the circle edges spluttered and sparked. All the circles shrank a little.

"Gazillion went through that one," Nine said, peering through the green circle. In the distance, she could see the crowded field of the Hopscotch Championship, with the fiery grid still glowing. "Do we follow?"

"The Stone answered 'blue'," said Flabberghast. He went over to the blue circle and stared.

Nine wandered over to the yellow circle. The House! Red as a strawberry, roof tiles falling off, shaking violently from side to side.

"The House is in the yellow circle!" said Nine. "It's not exploded yet! There's still time—"

"The Stone answered 'blue'," repeated Flabberghast, "and as unreasonable as it has become, I do not think it speaks untruths."

"But..." Nine walked away from the yellow circle – away from the House – doubts stabbing her over and over. She stood beside Flabberghast, who still cradled Spoon, and peered inside the blue circle. There was only blackness.

"It would free everyone?" She thought of the gargoyle and the promise she'd made, but more than anything, she thought of the pair of yellow eyes, staring from a stone.

She swallowed hard. "So, we jump in the yellow circle and return to the House. Or we jump through the blue circle into pitch blackness and probably certain death."

In that strange moment at the top of the Tower, Nine looked at Flabberghast and realised he had a small smile on his face.

"Yes," Flabberghast said, tucking Spoon closer to his chest. "I believe that is a very accurate summary. After you, Madam?"

Nine smiled back. "Together?"

Flabberghast nodded. "For Eric."

"For Eric," whispered Nine.

And so together, they leapt through the blue circle and into darkness.

Jumping through total blackness was a strange thing. Nine *thought* she was possibly falling, but she couldn't see or hear anything to confirm that. She *thought* it was taking a long time to be possibly falling, but then Time possibly didn't exist. Maybe it really was the End of Time.

Then suddenly, Time caught up with itself.

There was a whoosh of air – a rush of panic – as Nine realised, yes, she was falling and, no, she couldn't stop. A scream formed in her throat, but before it had a chance to come out...

Nine stumbled forwards and burst out of the oddly un-there place. Everything became sharp and focused again. She looked back and realised she had stepped out of the gold, swirly-framed not-a-mirror, and was back in the room where they'd started. Flabberghast was kneeling on the floor, still cradling Spoon in his arms. The five-pronged candlestick stood in the middle of the gloomy room, still with only one rainbow-coloured candle burning.

"I think, on the whole," Flabberghast said, looking nauseous, "I prefer the stairs." He reached up his pyjama sleeve.

"Yours, I believe, Madam." He pulled out Nine's music box and handed it to her.

Nine stared at the music box and then at the wizard. So many thoughts, so many feelings … and not a single word she could say… She simply took it and clasped it in her hand. Then she looked at the wizard and hoped her eyes said what her voice could not.

Flabberghast staggered to his feet. "Now why in the name of strawberry tea are we back in the room of mirrors?"

Nine shrugged and walked over to the candlestick. "What can we do here other than smash some glass? How will this free everyone?"

"I have no idea, Madam!" said Flabberghast, getting to his feet.

"The Asking Stone said blue," said Nine. She looked at the different mirrors in the dimly lit room: the rectangular not-a-mirror ... the black-framed oval one ... the dark, round one ... and the mirror decorated with golden question marks in the frame that was...

"Blue!" Nine said, pointing at the mirror.

"But – but how can we be sure?" asked Flabberghast.

"'Blue' was the only clue, and it brought us here. It must be to do with the mirror." said Nine. "We know these mirrors aren't quite what they seem."

They both moved in front of it and stared at their reflections and the unconscious Spoon. Nine breathed out. It steamed up as before.

"Should we smash it?" asked Flabberghast.

"But then the candle will go out," said Nine, "and I bet the Tower won't be happy about that."

"Well, what do we do, then? Gah!" Flabberghast grabbed handfuls of his hair. "Why did the Asking Stone have to leave us with so many questions?!"

"So many questions…" murmured Nine and stepped nearer to the mirror. She peered closely at all the gold question marks that ran around the blue frame. "But we only need one answer. Maybe one of these is different." She ran her fingers over the question marks – and gasped. Yes! One question mark was slightly raised. "This one!" she said to Flabberghast. "This one is different!"

Still cradling Spoon, Flabberghast leaned over to the question mark. "But we still don't know what to do. Wretched Tower!" he cried and pummelled his fist against the raised question mark.

Nine gasped as it popped out of the frame on a horizontal, metal stalk.

"Oho!" said Flabberghast. "I think we're rather getting the hang of this place, Madam!" He grasped the jutting-out question mark with his free hand and jiggled it furiously left and right.

There was a clonk as if a key had been turned in a lock, and the question mark pinged back into its upright position.

It was followed swiftly by a threatening rumble. The floorboards shook beneath Nine's feet.

"Flabberghast… What have you done?"

241

"Umm… I am not entirely sure, Madam."
He hastily pushed the question mark back into the mirror frame and held up his free hand in surrender.

Nine edged away from the question mark mirror, towards the candlestick. Then Nine heard the sound. A sound she'd almost forgotten, but one that pricked her heart with a thousand swords. The music box in her hand was whispering again. Like it had done when she had stood by the candles before.

The candles…

Burn. That's what the Tower had said.

Nine stared at the one remaining rainbow flame.

"Madam, we should leave!"

"No!"

Dust rained down from the ceiling. The walls shook. Small stones tumbled down around but Nine pushed the urgency from her mind. Her question. Finally, the answer to her question…

Her hand shook and she felt strangely sick as she dropped the music box onto the candle flame, hoping that this would work. Instead of being extinguished, the flame grew, as if it were devouring the little silver box.

The whispering grew louder … louder… Hardly daring to breathe, Nine stared into the darting, flickering flame.

CHAPTER 29

Was that ... a figure moving? In the rainbow flames?

The voice grew louder. It was tender and female.

"I'm sorry," said the voice. "I'm sorry, my darlin'. I have to leave you. I have no choice."

Nine just stared and stared at the image, because there, in the flame, was a face. A face she thought she knew. It belonged to a crouched figure, which looked out from the flame – and straight at Nine. For a moment, Nine forgot how to breathe. She reached her hand towards the flame.

"Ma," she whispered.

The figure turned aside and coughed painfully. "My darlin', this is the best place for you now.

Remember you are loved. Always. They'll take you in here. Care for you, clothe you, feed you." The figure smiled as tears rolled down her face. "Just remember ... one thing—"

"MADAM!" bellowed the wizard as a large stone fell towards Nine. She darted backwards, but it hit the candle stand and sent it crashing to the floor. The flame went out. The room went dark. There was the sound of a music box skidding across the room. And the whispering was silent.

"No!" screeched Nine, searching the ground in the darkness. "NOT YET! WHAT MUST I REMEMBER?"

No no no!

CRASH! As Nine's eyes grew accustomed to the gloom, she saw stones crumbling down from the ceiling, along with one of the wooden beams supporting it. Nine's fingers searched frantically through the rubble, sobs rising in her throat.

It must be here... It must be here...

Hands pulled her backwards. "NO!" cried Nine, shrugging Flabberghast off.

"YES!"

Flabberghast pulled her again, but her

fingertips brushed something. The music box!

She grasped it, stuffed it in her satchel, then pushed through the dusty fog. More stones smashed to the floor. Dust and grit rolled down. The sound of voices filled the staircase…

"Hurry!"

"Move along!"

"The Tower is crumbling!"

"All right! Going as fast as I can. Been stuck in a wall for two months!"

"Two years for me! I'll never get that purple sand out of my hair!"

Flabberghast opened the door and light flooded back into the room.

There was the sound of pushing and shoving as a frantic stream of unmazed, unwalled and unhourglassed witches and wizards bustled their way down the stairs towards the front door of the Tower. Nine grabbed Flabberghast's pyjama sleeve and pushed into the torrent.

"Come on," grumbled a gruff female voice Nine recognised. Something walked into the back of her knees. "Blimey, I ain't got all day."

"Eric? Eric?" Nine called, searching the endless

queue as it carried them down the steps and out of the front door.

As they piled out onto the grass outside, stones rained down from the shaking Tower. The throng of wizards and witches were all creating sparkling spirals with their fingertips and disappearing in colourful puffs of smoke.

"Where's Eric?" Nine scanned the crowd. "Eric?"

"Lady?" rumbled a voice. "LADY!"

Nine turned and saw the troll lumbering towards them. Her heart felt like it had been squeezed and, for a moment, the indescribable feeling seemed bigger than *she* was.

"Lady! Flabby!"

Eric broke into a clumsy trot and gave Flabberghast a huge hug, squashing the wizard's hat over his eyes. Then Eric released Flabberghast and went to pat Nine's head. He stopped halfway, uncertain...

But Nine turned to Eric, threw herself at him and gave him a big hug. The troll froze for a moment, as if he was wondering what had just happened. Then he beamed a wonky, tusky smile, and hugged her back.

For that moment, that one beautiful moment, Nine felt safe. But she pulled herself away awkwardly, shrugging him off.

"You," she said to Flabberghast. "Did you just break the Tower at the End of Time?"

Flabberghast opened his mouth to answer. As he did so, the whole Tower imploded with a roar. But as each stone fell down, it vanished, until there was nothing but the pointed stone tower top sitting on the grass, with an amber glow around it.

"Apparently so," said Flabberghast tightly.

HA! NO MORE QUESTIONS EVER AGAIN, muttered a voice from inside the tower top. TIME TO RETIRE BY THE SEA.

Suddenly the Asking Stone shot out of the roof, sending bricks and tiles scattering in every direction. The Stone spun wildly round and round as it shot upwards, becoming a small amber dot in the sky.

I'M TAKING UP STAAAAAAAAAMP COLLECTIIIIIIIIIING! said an increasingly distant voice in their heads. Then the Stone vanished in a puff of amber smoke.

They all stared at the remains of the demolished tower top.

Flabberghast grimaced. "Yes… I don't think I'm going to be terribly popular for a while."

The last few witches and wizards were starting to disappear.

"Come on," said Flabberghast. "Just grab hold of someone!" Tucking Spoon in closer, he took hold of the cloak of an elderly witch and they disappeared in a spiral of bright pink.

Nine clutched Eric's hand and ran towards a moody-looking young witch with stripy black and orange hair and an orange cloak. As the witch began lifting her hands up and shooting orange sparks, Nine grabbed the cloak.

"Hey! What the—?" began the witch, but her words were swallowed into nothing.

Nine felt all the air being sucked from her lungs. She clung desperately to the long-nailed hand behind her. She couldn't see, couldn't hear, couldn't think. Then just as she thought her head was going to explode from the weight of nothingness and everythingness, she felt herself spat out onto the ground. Back on the number ten.

CHAPTER 30

The golden, fiery markings of the hopscotch grid faded into nothing, leaving just white painted lines on the ground.

Noise roared around them. Fireworks burst into numbers in the air. Flags waved. Nine saw Gazillion dashing over the finish line by the judges' table, where the three judges sat. She scowled as he tossed his hair and flung wide his arms in victory. Witches floated by. Cheers rang out as witches and wizards were reunited.

Nine saw the little sapphire skull still there on the ground. She glanced around her, picked it up quickly and tucked it inside her satchel, touching her music box as she did so. Her music box... Those last words... *Just remember one thing...*

Her heart ached for her mother's unfinished words. As if something so very important was being held just out of sight, for ever gone. For ever unknown...

Flabberghast stood beside her, still cradling Spoon. "Madam!" he hissed urgently. "I think it unwise to linger in case they find out about the Tower."

Hundreds – maybe thousands – of wizards and witches milled about in the hopscotch arena, some seeming confused. Nine looked towards the judges. The message witch was staring in disbelief at the scene in front of her. She began frantically searching through the Scroll of Unbreakable Rules, presumably to check how many had just been broken. She unrolled armfuls of parchment until, with a defeated sigh, she tossed the entire scroll over her shoulder, where it landed with a satisfying thud.

"Come ON!" said Flabberghast, tugging Nine's arm. "To the House." They began pushing through the crowd.

"ATTENTION EVERYBODY FOR A VERY IMPORTANT ANNOUNCEMENT. EVERYBODY,

ATTENTION," droned the familiar voice from the red urn whizzing through the air in a slightly confused and panicked manner.

Nine looked over her shoulder as they pushed on towards the House. Ophidia stood up suddenly, dramatically swishing her emerald cloak back over her shoulders.

"Well, this is a most remarkable situation!" she boomed, gesturing to the packed arena. "Not only do I declare Gazillion the Unstoppable the winner of this year's Hopscotch Championship for returning first from the Tower at the End of Time, but also, I bestow upon him a special award for rescuing and returning our lost competitors!"

The crowd burst into deafening applause.

"What?!" said Nine and Flabberghast in unison. Flabberghast frowned as Gazillion raised his arms above his head in victory.

"Are you going to let him get away with that?"

"Yes, Madam," said Flabberghast, turning towards the House. "I am. Besides, I've rather lost the taste for hopscotch."

Nine watched as Ophidia leaned over the table and presented the deceitful wizard with a trophy. She watched as he whispered something in Ophidia's ear, and the witch's eyes lit up. But as Gazillion turned round, there was that same flicker of fear in his eyes. Then he stared at the crowd, quickly plastered on a smile, and waved his trophy in the air to another enthusiastic roar.

"Well, thank you all for coming," said Ophidia, hastily pushing back her chair. "Farewell."

"That's strange," said Nine, watching as the white-haired witch disappeared into the crowd in a flurry.

"Madam, it's hopscotch," said Flabberghast, pushing onwards. "It's meant to be strange."

"No, your aunt," said Nine.

"Madam, she's family," said Flabberghast. "*They're* always strange."

"But she and Gazillion seem to be up to something."

There was a swooshing noise behind them. Nine and Flabberghast whirled around.

"Oh, what joy awaits me," gloated Gazillion, appearing beside them. "Informing the Hopscotch Committee about you ruining the Tower whilst I managed to save all these poor souls! I doubt you'll ever play hopscotch again. Until our next meeting, Flabberghast the Unworthy." And he swished away into the skies.

"Can't wait," Flabberghast said through gritted teeth. "Oh! The House!"

There it was, red as a strawberry, shaking uncontrollably. One of the balconies was hanging off, and a sickly yellow-green steam burped out of the chimney every few seconds. As Flabberghast charged towards the House, knocking furiously on the front door, Nine looked up. Bonehead was at one of the windows, his bones all jiggling around with the force of the House's shaking. He gave a wobbly, jiggly double thumbs up. Nine waved back.

"Poor House," said Eric, his ears and tail drooping as he followed Flabberghast.

Something small crashed into her knees. Nine jumped and looked down.

"Oh," said a plump gargoyle with a gruff voice. "You again." Her face was exactly the same as it had been in the door – the frown, the oval eyes, the bulbous nose – but now she was a mottled grey colour and had wings and chunky, short legs. "You kept your promise. I'm impressed." She looked sharply at Nine. "Thanks."

"A promise is a promise," said Nine, as Flabberghast yelled and hammered on the front door. "What will you do now?"

"Well," said the gargoyle, "in a funny old way, the Asking Stone did answer me question. After years of being stuck in a wooden door, I ain't goin' back on a wall, watchin' the world as a waterspout, thank you very much. I'm off to explore."

The House hiccupped and the windows rattled. The hanging balcony drooped a little more.

"This your 'ouse? Bit of a state, ain't it?"

Nine sighed. "Tickling will stop the hiccups and let us in. But how – how do you tickle a House?"

"Blimey," said the gargoyle. "Don'tcha even know that? I tell you, when you spend your life sittin' on the walls of buildings, you can always guess rightly where a ticklish spot is."

Eric came lolloping back towards them.

"Can you guess where *this* house is ticklish?" Nine said, her hope rising.

"Course! Obvious, ain't it?" said the gargoyle.

"But I ain't got anythin' to tickle it wi—"

The gargoyle stopped as a feather duster was stuffed in her face. It was held in the hand of a beaming troll.

"Eric fix?"

Nine smiled. "Eric fix."

Nine watched as the gargoyle took the feather duster, put it between her teeth and started climbing up the wall of the House.

Flabberghast stopped pounding on the door and watched in amazement as the gargoyle swiftly and easily clambered up the brickwork, scaling a wooden pillar propping up the conservatory, before reaching above her for the ivy-like plant that crawled up the wall. From there, she headed for a little turret with an oval window jutting out on the right side of the wonky building. She removed the feather duster from her teeth and tickled the bricks.

A little giggle came out of the chimney.

Then there was silence.

No hiccups.

No shaking.

Just glorious, glorious silence.

CHAPTER 31

The silence lasted until Flabberghast began whooping. The strawberry-coloured House began returning to House-coloured House, from its middle outwards, to every balcony, roof tile and window ledge. And the front door sprang open.

In Flabberghast's arms, Spoon moaned. "I believe we need a cup of the Finest Tea in All the Realms," said Flabberghast. He skipped inside the House, followed by Eric.

"Thank you," said Nine, as the gargoyle jumped down and handed back the duster.

The gargoyle shrugged. "You scratch my back, I scratch yours."

Nine looked at her and smiled.

"What?" said the gargoyle. "Whatcha smilin' for?"

"Come with us," Nine said, pointing to the House. "We travel all the worlds *and* the World Between Worlds."

The gargoyle looked at the House, then at Nine. "Travel all the worlds, you say?"

"And you get a special room of your own." Nine smiled again. "And I promise it'll be *perfect* for you."

The gargoyle stroked her stony chin. "A room, eh? Beats sittin' on a wall bein' a waterspout. All right."

So, the two of them stepped inside the House, where Flabberghast waited in the hallway, and Eric stood on the doormat, holding the door open for them.

"More friend?" he said, smiling his wonky, tusky smile at the gargoyle.

"More friend," said Nine, and she gestured for the gargoyle to enter.

"The name's Cascadia Spout," said the gargoyle. "But 'stead of Cascadia, you can call me Cas."

"Well, that's handy," said Flabberghast, eyeing Eric. "Because a name with four syllables is really not going to work around here."

Cas stepped into the hallway.

"Welcome to the House at the Edge of Magic," said Flabberghast. He looked at Nine and raised an eyebrow.

Nine shrugged. "What? Sometimes we just pick up guests."

"We?" said Flabberghast.

"We." Nine unpinned the star-speckled cloak with one hand and threw it at the umbrella stand just inside the doorway. A blue arm shot up out of the stand, grabbed it and zoomed back inside again. Nine smiled. "It's good to be home." And she meant it.

Spoon moaned again, rubbed his head and sat up in Flabberghast's arms. He looked around the House, looked at the others and looked at his hand. "Where the devil's my sword?" he asked.

Nine and Flabberghast looked at each other.

"Ah. Dr Spoon. So glad you're feeling better. About your sword. We'll get you another one," said Flabberghast quickly, as Spoon groaned. "A better one. I know a very good blacksmith at the Back of Beyond."

"I should flamin' hope so," said Spoon. He

sat up a little straighter. "Beyond? That's where Professor Dish is!"

A look of realisation dawned on Flabberghast's face. "Then, Dr Spoon, I believe we have our next destination."

Eric took Spoon from Flabberghast and tucked him under his arm. "Make tea," he said, and lolloped down the hallway to the kitchen, with the gargoyle following behind. "Tea help."

"But, Flabberghast, you still haven't got your magic back," said Nine.

"No," said Flabberghast. "But I will, somehow. Preferably before we bump into Gazillion again."

Nine thought for a moment. "When you were in the Tower before, with your sister, and you asked your question, what did you ask?"

Flabberghast's eyes sparkled and he smiled knowingly. "Cup of the Finest Tea in All the Realms, Madam?"

Nine smiled back, as Flabberghast started walking down the hallway towards the kitchen. He stopped and called over his shoulder, "And if you'd be so kind as to do the honours..." He nodded at the shield by the front door.

Nine turned and put her hand on the toad's tongue on the shield. She gave it a sharp pull.

ZA-BAM! There was the strange feeling as though her brain were being sucked out of the top of her skull. Everything hurtled in a direction she didn't understand – but was possibly "up". But this time, she didn't feel so odd.

And so the House flew. Nine wobbled on the spot for a moment, then regained her balance. She pulled out the music box from her satchel. Nine swallowed hard, running the words over and over in her brain, wishing the music box had had a chance to finish its sentence. Nine burned the whispered words into her memory so she would never, ever forget.

The words her mother had spoken when she was three years old and sitting on a doorstep, wherever that was. *"I'm sorry, my darlin'. I have to leave you. I have no choice. This is the best place for you now. Remember you are loved. Always. They'll take you in here. Care for you, clothe you, feed you. Just remember one thing…"*

"Tea cupboard!" called Flabberghast from the kitchen.

ZAP! Nine was a closed fan with arms, still holding her music box. The fan flopped open with a picture of her mother's smiling face.

And with that extra surge of magic, the music box whispered for the very last time:

"...*never eat the pancakes.*"

Epilogue

In an un-hiccupping flying House, an excited young girl threw every question she could at the huggable troll and the ancient boy wizard. The same wizard who, many years ago, had once invited her mother to be their guest. The guest whose room Nine had discovered when she had climbed in the window that could never be shut...

For Nine's mother had not left her child abandoned in any old street doorway. She had placed her treasured music box in her daughter's hand and posted a letter through the letterbox mounted on the wall, knowing her dearest friends would take the child in. She had kissed the top of her daughter's head, knocked on the door and hidden round the side of the House, sinking to the ground, unable to watch, the words of her letter running through her mind…

Dear friends,

There's something important I need to tell you.

My days in the House at the Edge of Magic have been the best days of my life. But every journey must come to an end. Even the most extraordinary ones.

I know you'll take care of the most special thing I have in all the world.

And look after my music box, too. It means so much to me.

Please don't try to find me. You know I don't like saying goodbyes.

So, I'll just say thank you. For everything.

Eliza

But fate was against her. For Nine's mother had not noticed the whiskery gang-master in the shadows of the deserted alley, eyeing his latest prize. And she hadn't noticed the beautiful young lady with scarlet hair and ancient eyes watching from a window of the House as the events unfolded. The lady who would collect Eliza's letter as she whispered a single word: "Consequences."

No, Nine's mother noticed none of this. So when the front door opened and a puzzled, rumbly voice she adored said, "That odd," she did not know that he saw just an empty doorstep instead of her child, and that her daughter had already been stolen into the shadows.

And so, as the wall she leaned against vanished with the rest of the House, the mother smiled. Because she had given her child the most ridiculous, the most unbelievable, the most irritating, but the most perfect home she could possibly ever have...

The House at the Edge of Magic.

Acknowledgements

Firstly, a big thank you to everyone who has read this book, and *The House at the Edge of Magic*. It has been so wonderful to have your support and enthusiasm for this magical world. Every copy sold raises money for baby charity ICP Support, so thank you for helping to make a difference.

A book is always a team effort and I'm so thankful to have a magnificent team to work with. As always, a heartfelt thank you to my brilliant agent, Julia Churchill, who has somehow put up with me for over a decade. I banned her from reading any drafts of this book and resorted to secret communications via the Urn-to-Urn Messaging Service, so she wouldn't see the story until it was all finished and sparkly. Julia – I hope it was worth the wait! Thank you for being the Finest Agent in All the Realms.

A big thank you with pancakes on top to Gráinne Clear, my fabulous editor and partner-in-crime, for absolutely understanding this world, and for appreciating that there aren't many conversations that start, "Shall we put the Tower in the maze, or the maze in the Tower?" Gráinne, building this world with you is ridiculous fun, and I'm so glad there is more mischief-making to come!

To Miranda Baker for such eagle-eyed copy-editing. I really appreciate your hard work and clarity when I forget what colour a book cover is, who Spoon is threatening with a sword now, or which order numbers go in! Thank you for making sense of it all.

Thank you to Denise Johnstone-Burt, who fell in love with this series in the beginning and could see the potential in this crazy idea. Without her, this book wouldn't exist.

Huge thanks to Ben Mantle for yet another brilliant cover and illustrative work throughout the book. Ben, yet again you have done a marvellous job in bringing this all to life! Thanks also to Chloé Tartinville for the fantastic cover design, and to Rebecca Oram and the team for helping the book to get out there and spread mischief as widely as possible.

Special thanks to my long-suffering parents: Dad for encouraging me to write for older children in the first place, and to Mum, who not only adores this world, but sat up with me into the small hours as I faced mild peril (ok … deadlines), offering me chocolate as I wrote with an hourglass beside me.

I must also say a special thank you to my author friend, Kate Walker, who has been a tireless cheerleader in so many ways this year. I'm so glad our paths crossed!

And they may be last on the list, but they are first in my heart: much gratitude to my husband, Alyn, and our six children for tolerating my head being stuck in a Tower. Thanks for the tea and pancakes.

About the Author

Amy Sparkes studied English Literature and Theology at the University of Kent, and began writing after moving to Devon with her husband, six young children and an overactive imagination. Her books have appeared on CBeebies storytime and been shortlisted for several book awards, including the Roald Dahl Funny Prize and the BookTrust Best Books Awards for *Do Not Enter the Monster Zoo*. She runs author events for children, writing workshops for aspiring children's writers, produces the Writing for Children pages for bestselling *Writing Magazine*, and writes short stories for *Aquila* magazine. She co-founded the Writing Magazine Picture Book Prize and Chapter Book Prize for developing writers.

Are you enjoying the adventures of
Nine, Flabberghast, Eric and Spoon so far?

More coming soon…

We'd love to hear what you thought of
The Tower at the End of Time!

🐦 #TowerAtTheEnd
@WalkerBooksUK
@AmySparkes

📷 @WalkerBooksUK